Finding Suffolk Sam's Treasure

by Adie Copping

Copyright © 2021 Adie Copping

All rights reserved.

No part of this publication may be reproduced, stored in a retrieval system or transmitted in any form or by any means electronic, mechanical, photocopying, recording or otherwise, without the prior permission of the author.

Contents

Introduction 3
Glossary 5

The Grid of 39 7
First Stop ... Shotley 16
Pin Mill 25
Southwold, Here We Come . . . 32
Walberswick 42
Dunwich 46
Sizewell 51
Thorpeness 63
Aldeburgh 73
Snape 86
Orford 91
Woodbridge 104
Felixstowe Ferry and Bawdsey . . 116
Felixstowe 123
Landguard Point 139
Final Stop 147
Mixed photographs of locations . 151
Identity of photographs 164

Introduction

A book can be as simple as a cheese sandwich. Just throw together a few simple ingredients – bread, butter and cheese – and you can be quite content from the first bite to the last.

But, what if you feel the need for a lot more ingredients?

You may feel the need for a book on places to visit with a touch of history, and maybe, another book to while away a few relaxing hours on a short, humorous story. The short story could also involve a treasure trail around the region that could be followed by the reader if they desired. You may want to know more about the local accent and dialect too.

Well, this book you're now holding contains all of those ingredients above to create a sandwich with some extra taste that – hopefully – you will enjoy.

If you are holidaying visitor to Suffolk, and love exploring places along the coastline and its estuaries, then this book should give you some ideas on where to visit.

The short story involves taking you on a treasure trail journey through some of Suffolk's finest towns and villages with a trio of "Old Suffolk boys" with very differing characters; John, the calm, sensible and more intelligent one; Reg, the slightly gullible, and not quite so intelligent one, and George … well … abrupt, outspoken … the least said about him the better.

The story in this book has been written with just a touch of the Suffolk accent/dialect to give it some local flavour which some readers may find hard to follow at the very beginning. But, I assure you that after reading a few pages of words containing the letter i with an added o before them to create an "oi", such as in "Oi'm alroight," the flow will come much easier the further one gets into the book.

The written accent has been kept as simple as possible to help keep a good flow, if it was written with a full blown Suffolk accent most outsiders would find it a real struggle which would ruin the story.

For those of you that may wish to follow the trail and try and find the dates for yourselves, I've mixed up a selection of photos of the relevant places for you to confirm your findings. There is a list of their identity on the last page … I didn't want to make all of them too obvious. Have fun!

Note: The mast, Royal Naval training Establishment, HMS Ganges, Shotley.
   As at the time of writing, the mast on the grounds of the school was still in place – although in a very poor state of neglect – and could be seen from the entrance gate on the Caledonia Road/School Road junction.
   The site has planning for major re-development with the building of new residential homes after standing vacant for many, many years.
   Due to the mast having been such an historical landmark, the new landowners hope to have the mast fully restored to its original condition, which would be great for the people of Shotley and also great for all the many visitors that stop by in the area.

Glossary

To help make reading this book a little easier, here is a selection of words to be found within the text – some more obvious than others.

Oi ... I,	roight ... right	moind ... mind
Oi'm ... I'm,	moight ... might	moine ... mine
Oi'll ... I'll,	loight ... light	moiles ... miles
Oi'd ... I'd,	soight ... sight	moight ... might
Oi've ... I've	foight ... fight	asoide ... aside
Troiy ... try	boiy ... by	boike ... bike
Couz ... because	agin ... again	

Wha' ... what	wha's ... what's	tha' ... that
Bin ... been	sin ... seen	bein' ... being
Git ... get	dint ... didn't	hent ... haven't
Hev ... have	hed ... had	huum ... home
Hevin' ... having	tew ... to/too	dew ... do
Yew ... you	yit ... yet	'en ... then

T'git ... to get   t'day ... today   yisterdee ... yesterday
Realoise ... realise remoind ... remind   droive ... drive
Arternuun ... afternoon   anuvver ... another

Int ... am not, and can also mean, haven't ("Oi int gonna dew it!", or "Int yew done tha' yit?").

Note: A lot of Suffolk folk don't sound the letter 'T' at the end of their words, so for this book only a few common words is written without. If all the text was written without the 'T's' in place it would make for extremely difficult reading.

The Grid of 39

'Don't even think about it, George.'

'– Think about wha', John?'

'Oi could see ya eyeing up moiy roast tater couz yew've eaten all o' yours.'

'Oi moight've thought about it.'

'There weren't no moight've. If someone hed come through tha' door and oi'd looked round at 'em, it would've gone –' and at that precise moment, the latch clicked loudly open on the pub door and in walked their friend Reg, with a big smile on his face, 'Arternuun boys,' he said as he looked around the room.

Clutching an ominous looking black book in his right hand, Reg made his way over to the bar, 'Usual please Moichael,' giving barman Michael, a nod and a wink.

'And anuvver,' quickly called out George, with a raised mug and munching a mouthful of roast potato.

'Yew swoine, George,' growled John, having just noticed that his last potato had vanished.

'Jan's roast taters, uuumm, wha' can oi say … irresistible!' George replied, licking his fingers one by one. John was not amused.

'He int up tew his old tricks agin is he, John?' asked Reg as he watched Michael top up the first beer. 'Oi lost foive pounds in weight in a week heving meals with him when moiy missus hed t'go in t'hospital – never agin.'

'Yew two are carrying tew many pounds anyway. The ladies take a loiking to a trim looking fella loike me,' said George trying to look sauve.

'Well they wouldn't be tew happy about yew nicking their taters if they were on the plump soide, would they mate!' John retaliated, still fuming over his stolen potato.

Reg wandered over with the beer and placed it on the table before going back for the book.

'Wha' ya got there 'en Reg, ya little black book with your old flames phone numbers innut?' George smirked.

On returning to the table, Reg gave George the slightest of grins then pulled out a chair, sat down, and laid the book on the table. It had barely made contact with the table when George snatched it away for a look. Reg just looked nonchalantly at John, took a sup of beer and didn't say a word.

George flicked through the pages expectantly, hoping to find some dirt on Reg, but he was soon disappointed. 'Wha's this all about with these drawings of ol' mansions and stuff?' he muttered, 'yew got an interest in old houses or something?'

'Oi want tew pick ya brains,' said Reg, as he looked at both John and George in succession. 'Oi can't make head no tail of the thing – never could.'

As John reached over to take the book and have a look for himself, Reg started to reveal the story about the book.

'Oi was sorting out me bookshelf this mornin' and come across it then. Oi'd forgotten all about it. Oi've hed it for years. Anyway, it was given tew me by this ol' boy oi knew, Suffolk Sam, just a few days before he pegged it.'

'Suffolk Sam?' retorted George. 'Wha' sort of a name is Suffolk Sam?'

'Everyone knew him as Suffolk Sam, couz he would never go outside the county. He once told me it was something tew dew with the law, them in Essex was always on his back so he never went over the other side of Stour estuary anymore. Oi don't know what that was all about, oi never asked.'

'A dodgy bloke then,' George remarked.

'Nah – not Sam, he was a noice ol' boy. Other folk avoided him for some reason but oi couldn't see whoiy, me an' him used tew git on loike a house on fire. Oi used tew visit him a lot and he would tell me all his adventures he had on his boat all along the coast.'

'Adventures!' laughed George, 'He was a poirate was he?'

Reg just ignored George completely and continued with the tale while John sat studying the book of drawings and handwritten work in great detail.

'He was a funny ol' boy,' Reg continued, 'he used tew talk in riddles a lot of the toime –'

'No wonder yew got on with him alroight 'en,' interrupted George, 'sounds loike yew two were two of a koind – we don't know wha' yew're on about half the toime.'

'As oi was a sayin': oi can remember him one toime sayin' t'me somethin' about his sprouts were feeling bad after an accident with a garden rake – tha' sort of thing. But oi couldn't see any sprouts in his garden; tha' dint make any sense t'me.'

John and George just burst out laughing. 'Oi dunno – he's a one, int he John?' laughed George.

'Wha' …?'

'Never moind Reg, just carry on,' said John. 'If this book is anything tew go boy, he certainly was an interesting bloke!'

'Really?' beamed Reg.

'Really!' replied John looking very serious. 'Wha' did he dew for a livin'?'

Reg paused for a moment and looked up to the ceiling in thought, 'Oi don't roightly know. All oi know was that he had a boat for years and years which he moored at Pin Mill.'

'Wha' sort of a boat?' asked John.

'A small fishin' boat oi s'pose, it had an engine that chugged along real noice loike. He took me up the river a few toimes and we would stop off at Shotley and hev a couple a pints in the Bristol Arms there. They were great days. A long toime ago now,' smiled Reg.

'How long ago was this 'en and how long hev yew hed this book?' asked John.

Reg looked up at the ceiling again, 'Cor ... it must be ... 1980, tha's roight, 'couz oi can remember him bein' 80 at the toime –'

'Wha'!' exclaimed John *'yew've had this book for 40 years and didn't know what it was all about?'*

'No – oi still don't. When he gave it tew me he said, "this book will make yew a lot of money but yew've got tew earn it. Study every page" he said, something about him hevin' earnt it the hard way and oi needed t'use moiy head more. But yew know me ... oi'm no good with complicated things – so oi put it asoide.'

'Was he rich?' asked George.

'Oh no, he weren't rich but he always hed plenty of money boiy the look of things ... he loiked his whiskey ... he was always drinkin' that ... he hed a noice little cottage tew.'

'Dew yew know anything about all these mansions and big houses in this book, did he use t'say anything about them?' asked John.

'Well he did, but oi can't remember much about it now couz it was so long ago. He did hev a thing about 'em saying how they generated such beauty with all foine things tha' only rich people could afford. Oi can remember him tellin' me somethin' loike, wha's the word now ... majestic, tha's roight; majestic – how majestic they looked boiy day and how calm and asleep they looked boiy moonloight. He hed a way with words he did.'

'Moonloight – how many ordinary folk get the chance t'see these big houses boiy moonloight, oi ask ya?' remarked John. 'Boiy the look of this book oi'd say tha' Suffolk Sam led a devious loifestyle yew dint know about, Reg!'

'Wha' d'ya mean boiy tha' John?'

'Oi'm pretty sure he was a bloomin' burglar, he robbed these places. It's as plain as ya face when yew look through these pages!'

'D'ya reckon tha's what he was?' George said excitedly. 'Let me hev another butchers at tha' book a minute!'

Reg quietly shook his head in total disbelief, 'Naow, no, no, no, not Sam, he was a noice ol' boy he weren't no burglar, he couldn't hev bin.'

'Wha' dew ya think all his adventures were?' remarked George. 'He weren't going t'tell ya t'ya face exactly what he got up tew, was he. No wonder folk who knew him avoided him, they probably knew he was dodgy – tha's whoiy yew and him got on so well, couz he knew yew were soft enough not to cotton on!'

'Oh, well thank yew very much –!' sarcastically replied Reg, feeling a touch offended.

'George dint mean anything boiy it, Reg,' intervened John, 'But yew know yew're a bit gullible at toimes ... well ... a lot of the toime really.'

'Look at these in here,' said George as he flicked through the pages and pointed out notes at the bottom of each drawing of a house; 'Dogs ... no dogs ... geese ... dogs ... gamekeeper ... dogs ... no 'd or g' – oi s'pose tha's no dogs or geese. Whoiy would anyone wroite tha' down? Oi think ya roight John, he's cased these places so he knew how tew deal with'em.'

'Did he own a car, Reg?' asked John.

'No – he only hed a pushboike tha' he used t'git down tew his boat on. He used to put it in his boat to keep it safe –' then Reg started to laugh. 'Yew two are gettin' silly now. He was just an ordinary bloke who worked on the river in his little boat and happened t'loike houses and all tha' arky ... checkchur stuff – yew know wha' oi mean.'

'Architecture, Reg, architecture. Wait a minute ... give me back tha' book a minute George,' asked John with some urgency.

John quickly flicked through the pages and muttered the names of the houses as he went through it; 'Woolverstone Hall ... Freston House ... Wherstead Mansion ... Woodhall Manor ... Seckford Hall ... Henham Hall ... just look at all these in here, yew two. Hev ya noticed tha' there's a pattern here. Just about all of these houses are in close proximity of the rivers and harbours all the way up the coast. He could moor up his boat close boiy; rob the places and quoietly slink off out of soight across the waters. He could even use his boike for those a little further inland!'

Reg just sat there shaking his head with his arms folded while George, supping his beer, kept peering across at the book as John flicked through the pages.

At half distance through the book there were no more entries, just blank pages, but John continued through anyway just for his own curiosity.

With about twenty or so pages left to go, John found some more handwriting, but this time it was written close to the join of the pages from top to bottom, covering no more than a third of the page either side. George could see that John had found something.

'Wha's all tha' there John?' George asked, as he queried the writing, 'Tha's a funny way tew wroite in a book.'

John quietly muttered as he started to recite the writing: "They say travel broadens the mind, find the answers and the stash you will find. Follow the path in order to the book or you'll never be on track for the right place to look."

'That sounds loike a treasure trail, John,' George remarked.

John turned to the next page and there again was more writing close to the join: "Add up the numbers of the dates that you see, and the words will be revealed on the grid one, two, three."

'It *is* a treasure trail, John. But wha's the grid thing all about?'

'Steady on George, one thing at a toime. We'll get there in a minute.'

'Dew ya believe it now, Reg?' said George, trying to convince Reg that it was true. 'It's all there. The stash it said. The ol' boiy told yew the book would make yew rich, so it's got t'be stolen goods he's hidden up. Yew've gotta accept it mate, there's no doubt about it, he was a burglar – he weren't an antique dealer tha's for sure!'

Reg, in a mild state of shock, just sat staring at his pint of beer with this new found revelation, and shook his head in disbelief, 'Oi just can't believe it. After all these years you're tellin' me ... oh ... oi can't believe it ... he was just loike a granddad t'me and all the toime he was ... well ... a criminal ya tellin' me?'

'Probably a long, long, retired criminal when yew knew him Reg,' consoled John.

John read out some more writing from another page: "A ships mast so tall stands at Ganges, Shotley Gate, you'll find the year it was planted there but it was not noineteen o eight." Well we all know there's a mast there – who doesn't? But when it was put there is a diff'rent matter.'

'But where's tha' grid, John?' George asked impatiently, 'If there int no grid it's all pointless!'

John flicked over more pages with more and more verses tucked in deep to the join, 'Yew know whoiy these hev bin written near the join don't ya?'

George and Reg looked at each other without a clue and then looked back at John with anticipation.

'Well, when folk quickly look through a book, most will bend a whole a bunch of pages an' let 'em flick quickly through off ya thumb, tha' way ya wouldn't see the wrotin' here near the join. Tha's whoiy me an' yew missed it the first toime we looked. If someone else had found this book they'd hev probably missed it tew. But when Reg said earlier that Sam said "study every page", it's just luck tha' oi did.'

John continued turning the pages and with no more than six pages to go, the grid they were looking for appeared before them. There were thirteen rows of words with three random words per row, numbered one to thirty nine.

1	East	2	On	3	Church
4	West	5	Steps	6	Under
7	The	8	House	9	Left
10	Boat	11	Shed	12	Floor
13	Yule	14	Find	15	Treasures
16	Tree	17	Galore	18	Part
19	Stone	20	Lead	21	Dig
22	By	23	Lace	24	Is
25	Neither	26	Sea	27	Paces
28	Down	29	Seven	30	Straight
31	Up	32	Nor	33	North
34	River	35	Cross	36	Room
37	The	38	Place	39	Wall

John twisted the book round so they all could see the grid of words and as they all leaned over the table and peered at the selection, each one of them quietly muttered different words that had caught their eye.

'Well boiys,' said John holding up his mug of beer, 'Oi don't know about yew George, but oi think we're gonna be takin' Reg on a treasure trail – are yew both free tomorra?'

'Tew roight we bloomin' are!' replied George, and with a clatter of mugs, smiles and nods all round, it was eyes down once again as they continued investigating more pages of Suffolk Sam's book.

First Stop ... Shotley

The next day, George pulled up in his car at John's house where he found Reg already waiting outside in the front garden. The three of them had agreed to start the trail close to home as they were all overly keen to find some dates and see what words they could bag from the grid.

'John will be out in a minute, George. He's just strainin' his greens afore we set off.'

Within a few seconds John appeared out of the front door shaking his head, 'Thank yew, Reg, oi'm sure moiy neighbours appreciate yew makin' a public announcement of moiy bodily functions!'

'Oi was just puttin' George in the picture. Ya know how impatient he can be when he's sittin' in his car.'

'Roight – well, we're all set t'go then. Let's hope Stirlin' Moss has a loighter foot than he had the last toime oi got in the car with 'im – oi'm sure moiy hair went a loighter shade of grey tha' last trip out oi hed with him.'

John and Reg got into the car to find George in a very excitable mood, 'Welcome aboard me hearties,' he said in a typical pirate tone. 'Tis the day we go huntin' for unimaginable treasures.'

'Unimaginable might be the roight word. For all we know George, there moight not be any,' said John trying to quell George's enthusiasm in the hope of some steady driving.

'Yew can't say tha' John, we're only just startin' out. This moight be the most excitin' thing any of us has ever done before –'

'Well, oi'm excoited,' quickly remarked Reg with a beaming smile.

'Oi'm not one for troiyin' to put a damper on thing's but we've got to be realistic here, tha's all,' said John softly. 'Oi was thinkin' last noight that forty years have passed on and who knows what moight've happened in tha' toime – someone else moight already hev stumbled across it. And on top of that, if we do foind it, there moight not be that much there anyway. Oi really can't imagine a little ol' bloke of eighty havin' stashed away a hoard of stuff and not fenced most of it all off ...'

'Well p'rhaps he thought he was gonna live tew a hundred,' interjected George.

'Meanin' wha' exactly?'

'Well, he moight have pawned stuff off gradually t'pay his bills and the loike and hed enough stuff t'last him til he was a hundred. He weren't t'know he was gonna peg it at eighty, did he!'

John raised his eyebrows on the possibility, 'Well, yew moight hev a point there oi must admit.'

'He did hev a friend who was a pawnbroker,' piped up Reg. 'He used t'see him regular loike ... gotta a place in Ipswich, somewhere?' Both John and George turned round in their seats, surprised at the unexpected statement, *"Yew what?"* they both asked in unison.

'Well tha' says it all then!' said John. 'Tha's more or less confirmation tha' he certainly was a burglar. Whoiy dint yew tell us tha' afore?'

'Oi weren't t'know yew wanted t'know that. Oi dint think of it until George said about pawnin' stuff.'

'Can yew remember his name?' asked John.

'Ooo, let me think ... it was a weird name,' replied Reg with a skyward look, 'it was ... tha's roight, it was Stan – definitely Stan.'

'Stan?' queried George with a puzzled look.

'Tha's roight – it was Stan.'

'Wha's so *weird* about the name Stan?' asked George curiously.

'Oh no, not that name, oi was thinkin' of another name before oi remembered it bein' Stan, tha's all,' explained Reg with a scratch of the head.

'Wha' was this Stan fella's surname?' asked John.

'Ooo – oi've got no idea.'

'Well, wha' was the name of the pawnbrokers 'en?'

'Ooo – no idea about tha' one either.'

'Dew ya know what street it was on?'

'Ooo – it was ... wait a minute ... no, no ... sorry, no idea.'

'Roight,' said a bemused John, 'oi've hed enough of this conversation, let's get gorn before moiy head starts hurtin'. George – onward t'Shotley, and let's get this thing started.'

With a rolled eyed look at John, George started the car and off they set.

On reaching Shotley Gate, they drove down the hill to see the River Stour before them with the town of Harwich across the water in the distance beyond. As they turned left to head to the marina they passed the Bristol Arms pub.

'Are we stoppin' for a pint afterwards?' asked Reg. 'Oi int bin in there for a long, long whoile.'

'Oi think we'd better pass on tha', this toime Reg,' replied John, 'Oi thought we'd drop in at the Butt an' Oyster when we drop back tew Pin Mill after this. Ya gotta remember tha' George is droivin', so we want t'keep him with a clear head, don't we?'

'A clear head for wha'?' asked George, giving John a long, serious look.

'Ya droivin' of course ... LOOK OUT, GEORGE!' yelled John, and within that very next second, the car bounced violently up in the air as it hit a traffic calming, speed hump on the road, causing them all to leave their seats momentarily.

'*FLAMIN' PARSNIPS!*' cried George. 'Where did tha' come from ...?'

'Ya weren't lookin' where yew were gorn, were ya – yew were lookin' at me!' replied John, rubbing the top of his head. 'Are ya alroight back there, Reg?'

'Oi'm alroight,' he chuckled, 'oi thought it was roight funny couz oi saw it coming.'

'Oh thanks a lot, Reg!' sarcastically growled George. 'If next toime we happen t'be headin' towards a cliff yew'll let me know won't ya, couz tha' would be *real funny tew,* wouldn't it!'

Reg just quietly chuckled to himself ignoring George's moment of anger as he knew that his bark was often a lot worse than his bite, but he still had to tread carefully as George would often let loose with his mean streak when least expected.

Further along the road another hump could be seen in the distance and Reg thought he'd risk winding up George some more, 'Don't forgit the hump ahead, George!'

'*Oi can see it, oi can see it!*' cried George sternly, as he got even more rattled.

But while Reg found it highly amusing, John sat there tight-lipped thinking that Reg was pushing his luck.

Several hundred yards and a few more humps later they arrived at the car park to the marina and parked up overlooking the large stretch of water over to the Felixstowe docks. From the left, the River Orwell flows into the bay and meets with the River Stour that flows from the right. With just over two miles of water stretching over to Landguard Fort on the far side, it's quite a panoramic sight.

Harwich sits quietly to the right of the bay whilst to the left it's a busy world of giant cranes and enormous container ships.

All three got out of the car and walked up to the sea wall and surveyed the view before them.

'Oi'd loike t'go up in one of those cranes,' remarked George, 'must be a helluva view from up there.'

'Must be,' replied John, 'When folk look across t'those they don't realoise how big they are.'

'Yew wouldn't git me up there!' Reg cringed, shaking his head. 'Me legs would be shakin' loike a fruit jelly.'

'Well, oi don't know what yew'd' hev done if yew were at this Ganges school behoind us in the day?' said George, as he turned round to look at the mound of land behind them that once belonged to the navy training school. 'Come on – let's go foind wha' we've come here for, we int got all day.'

Behind some freestanding, dry docked yachts the Ganges museum awaited them with volumes of information on the history of the school.

As they walked towards the door, John again reminded them of the verse in the book: "A ships mast so tall stands on ground at Shotley Gate, the year it was planted there was not noineteen o eight."

As soon as they stepped inside the door, George is drawn to a photograph of the famous mast where the boys of the school were lined along the yardarms all the way up to the very top, 'Here ya are Reg,' said George with a devious grin, 'How d'ya reckon ya legs would've felt up on tha' begger – and what about the one on top, look at him, cor?'

'Ooo, oi feel all funny just lookin' at it!'

'One hundred and forty three foot hoigh, tha's bloomin' hoigh – yew'd hev wet y'self up there, Reg,' chuckled George.

'Can ya remember tha' Blew Peter bloke gorn up it years back, wha's his name now ... John Noakes, tha's it. Better him than me. He was a brave sod he was – or a bloomin' daft one, which ever way ya want t'look at it. Health and safety wouldn't allow anythin' loike that nowadays.'

'He went up Nelson's Column tew,' remarked John as he peered at another photograph, 'that was tew clean the pigeon crap of it, oi think? The thing's he would do for the BBC – remarkable fella was John,' continued John. 'Anyway lookey here ... oi've found wha' we're lookin' for. It says here the mast was originally from HMS Cordelia, a ship built in eighteen eighty one. The mast was taken off it when it was sold in noineteen o foive and then it was erected here in Shotley in, wait for it ... noineteen o seven.'

'Wa'hey – erected, planted, stuck in the ground, whatever – we're on our way Reg!' cheered George as he rubbed his hands together with glee. 'What word does it give us on the grid, John?'

'Its early days yet, George – oi don't think we need worry tew much about tha' roight now, we've got a stack of other date's t'foind as yet, so it int gonna help us much is it?'

'Oi wanna know ...' insisted George like some small child.

'Oh for goodness sake, if it's gonna make ya happy!' tutted John.

'Well he int the only one,' piped up Reg, 'oi'd loike t'know tew – after all, it is moiy treasure we're huntin' –'

'Your treasure ...! Oh it's your treasure now is it?' George scowled, 'If it weren't for –'

'Shhhhh!' John quickly interjected with a finger to his lips, 'yew daft sods, dew yew want everyone in here t'know about it? At the moment it int anybody's, we've got t'foind it first and if we don't foind it, well ... that's that. But, if we *are* fortunate enough t'foind it we'll cross tha' bridge when we come tew it, alroight. Now let's go outsoide and oi'll hev a look at the grid and foind this one word tha's *so* important tew ya both roight now.'

They made their way out of the museum door in a tight huddle creating a few puzzled glances from others in there, especially the curator who then watched them eagle-eyed through the window, not sure what they were up to.

John took out the book from a large pocket on his fisherman's jacket and then flicked through the pages to find the grid of words, 'Here we are – let's see. Nineteen o seven makes one add nine, ten plus seven, that's seventeen.'

He then slid his finger up to the seventeenth word and pointed it out to George and Reg, to see for themselves.

'Galore ...' muttered George quietly. 'Tha's a funny word to start with, int it?'

'Happy now?' asked John with a hint of sarcasm.

'Oh yeah – we've gotta be haven't we?' George replied with a dead serious look. 'It's our first word int it. It's a start. We've got one under our belt. We should be happy. Aren't yew happy, Reg?'

'Roightly so,' replied Reg with a nod of the head.

'Roight then,' said John, 'we'd better make a little grid of our own and then we can wroite the word "galore" in the roight place and then hev it ready for all the other words.'

Again George rubbed his hands together at the thought of the riches at the end of the trail.

'Flippin' heck, man!' said John rolling his eyes, 'if ya rubbin' ya hands that hard at this stage George, they'll be catchin' fire before we foind the rest of the words! 'Come on, let's head back tew Pin Mill and then we can all hev a pint.'

After some nods of agreement, they all clambered back into the car and set off for the return drive over the road humps where again Reg couldn't help himself but to try and annoy

George for the second time, 'Moind the hump, George,' he grinned. But George didn't bat an eyelid.

As they rounded the turn at the Bristol Arms and headed uphill, George was keen to have a look at the mast that was still standing at the top of the road.

'Just a sloight detour tew the roight when we git t'the top,' he said grinning with a quick look back at Reg. 'Oi jus' wanna see the mast again and imagine Reg standin' on the button at the top.'

'Dew we have tew?' replied Reg looking sheepish.

'Yeaaah, it'll only take a couple of minutes. Crikey's boiy, oi int askin' ya t'cloimb it!'

They took the turn right and pulled up at the locked gate at the end of the road. Inside the grounds some 50 yards away to the left, stood the mast. As it was only a quick visit, George temporarily left the car engine running while they all got out of the car for a better look.

'Cor – they must've hed some nerve t'cloimb tha' thing in the day – especially when yew think, these lads were all about fifteen years old at the toime,' commented George.

'Ah yeah, but remember at that age a lot were fearless, they didn't see the real danger,' replied John. 'It int til yew git as old as us tha' yew realoise how dangerous it was!'

'It's no good oi'm gittin' back in the car?' said Reg, looking pale in the face. 'Oi feel peculiar with yew two jus' talkin' about it.'

George started to laugh and pointed at Reg's legs, 'Look at 'im, oi can see his legs shakin' from here and tha's with both his feet on the ground!'

'Oi can't help it, can oi!' cried Reg, getting a little agitated. 'Oi've jus' got a vivid imagination and oi don't loike height's, alroight!'

'Alroight, alroight, Reg, come on – just ignore him,' said John, trying to deflate the jibes, 'Its loike spendin' toime with Laurel and Hardy with yew two hevin' a go at each other all the toime. George – not another word! Come on let's get gorn tew the Butt and Oyster.'

Pin Mill

After a few quiet miles along the winding road to Chelmondiston, Reg breaks the silence with one of his "think out loud" thoughts that he would randomly often do. 'Oi wonder if there's any squirrels out there tha' git vertigo …?'

George looked across at John and rolled his eyes before quietly remarking, 'Here we go agin, John.'

'Oi mean; if humans can hev these phobia's whoiy can't animals. Surely there must be a squirrel or two out there tha' git the jitters about cloimbin' a tree … and what about rabbits?'

'Rabbit's – wha' are yew on about now, Reg, they don't cloimb trees?' stated John in confusion.

'Oi know they don't cloimb trees, oi was jus' thinkin' tha' some moight git clods-treephobia, oi can't see whoiy they couldn't.'

'Reg, the word is claustrophobia, and oi very much doubt any rabbit tha's born and brought up in a burra is gonna hev claustrophobia!' George just burst out laughing and drifted across the road very slightly which was just enough to unnerve John. '– Jus' look where ya gorn, George, or we'll be joinin' the rabbits in the hedgerow in a minute! Lets forget about squirrels and bloomin' rabbits for the moment and let me foind the next verse for us all, so tha' one of us moight spot the date on the way down tew the pub.'

John, again opened up the book and flicked through the pages to find the appropriate verse to recite: "The first letter of the Greek alphabet is written on the wall, go back up the hill and a dwellin' will reveal all."

'Well, we all know tha' Alpha is the letter 'A', don't we?' said George.

'Do we?' replied Reg. 'Oi don't know anythin' about Greek stuff – oi never did loike history at school. All they ever talked about was old stuff.'

'Dint ya learn some of it when yew hed English lessons?' George queried.

'Oi dint loike tha' either!' replied Reg shaking his head.

'Did ya loike geography?' asked John.

'Nope ...'

'Wha' about art?' continued John.

'Nope ...'

'Was there *anything* ya loiked at school?'

'Oh yeah ...'

'Wha' was tha' then?'

'Sharon Smedworth.'

'Oh very funny Reg ...' grinned John shaking his head, 'so ya dint loike gorn t'school 'en?'

'Oh, oi dint moind gorn t'school, and oi dint moind gorn huum – it was the bit in the middle oi dint loike!'

Both John and George shook their heads and grinned at one another. 'So you're not the best educated old duffer in town then Reg?' asked George wryly.

'Oi don't s'pose oi am ... tha's whoiy oi couldn't understand wha' tha' book was all about – moiy brain can't handle certain things.'

'Never moind, Reg,' said John, 'oi'm sure yew make up for it in other ways.'

There was a pause as Reg thought for a moment, then said cheerfully, 'Oi'm good at bakin' cakes.'

'Well there yew go 'en, Reg, there hed t'be somethin'!' replied John, giving George a quick wink.

At that moment they arrived at Chelmondiston, and just a few hundred metres later, George flicked the indicator for the right turn ahead, 'Here we go boiys, the pub is beckonin', oi can smell moiy pint o' beer from here,' he said with a lapping sound from his tongue.

The road narrowed as they made their way down the half mile or so of the lane, and as they reached the final one hundred metres, houses appeared to their right.

'Dead slow here, George,' said John as they travel slightly downhill, 'we moight see a date on the way down.'

As they rounded a gentle bend, the mile wide river came into view with a large mudflat to the fore as the tidewater had long receded to the sea. A pair of tired barge hulls rested on the mud creating an image of an old world with a slower pace of life that had long gone.

As George eased the car slowly down the hill, all eyes were scanning feverishly for anything that related to the verse from the book, but nothing could be spotted.

'Nah ... this is no good,' commented John, 'we can't see things properly loike this. It'll be better out of the car and walkin' it. Park the car behind the pub George and we'll go and hev a proper look.'

Once the car was parked, the lads got out and made their way back to the road to walk back up the hill. 'Oi'm doiyin' for a pint, boiys!' remarked George as he watched a few customers downing their drinks on the nearby benches. 'We've got plenty of toime for tha',' replied John. 'Hopefully this shouldn't take tew long.' And he wasn't wrong, as it was no more than forty or so paces up the road that they found what they were looking for.

'There it is!' said George, pointing with his finger, '"Alpha Cottage", it says.'

Where most of the houses were parallel with the road, this particular red bricked cottage faced the river and had a weather-worn central plaque inscribed, "Alpha Cottage, 1898".

'Oi only just spotted tha' – it doesn't, exactly stand out real clear loike, does it? "Eighteen noighty eight" – tha's wha' we're lookin' for int it, John?'

'Oi reckon it must be, it's the only thing round here with the word Alpha on it.'

'Tha's two in the bag already – this is fun!' beamed Reg, as he pulled out his wallet from his pocket and waved it at the lads. 'Toime for a pint oi reckon!'

George's eyes lit up as Reg was never the swiftest for paying for the first round of drinks, 'Flippin' Nora, John, oi think oi need t'sit down roight quick – oi've come over all funny with the shock!' he said as he put on an act of dizziness.

'We'd better get down there quick before he changes his moind – come on!' jokingly added John with a smile.

In no time at all, all three of them were sat on a pub bench supping their pints and surveying the quiet, timeless world that makes Pin Mill so special – the scenic view of the river to the right with a scattering of boats and yachts – the sound of the black and white oyster catchers whistling loudly as they fly nearby – to the fore, a mix of cottages and boats, with boat owners working on their crafts just outside the small boatyards – a tiny stream trickling past the front of the small green in the centre of it all.

'So wha' word hev we got this toime, John?' asked George.

'Hold on a minute – oi moight as well tell ya everytoime couz ya gonna keep askin' whatever. Let me see … it was eighteen nointy eight so tha's one an' eight makes noine an' noine an' eight makes seventeen, tha' makes it twenty six, yeah?'

'Oi made it twenty seven,' replied George.

'How'd ya come tew tha' then?' asked John looking puzzled.

'Well, one an' eight is noine; then there's the next noine an' yew git another noine when ya add the one from the front tew the last eight so there's three noines – twenty seven.'

'Three noines …? Yew used the one, twoice, ya puddin'!'

'Did oi? Oo – wait a minute, oi did dint oi. Oi reckon me brain must be startin' tew malfunction loike Reg's!'

'Yew wha'! Wha' d'ya mean, startin' t'malfunction?' sharply replied Reg.

'Oi'm only jokin', Reg!' grinned George.

'Anyway,' said John quickly intervening, 'Twenty six gives us the word … "sea".'

"Sea," said George, 'Tha' could mean anythin'.'

'Well, it could well dew, but we'll hev t'wait and see wha' goes with it, shant we.'

As the three of them continued drinking, they watched a man climb up a ladder onto a hull of a rough looking boat that was is in the process of being renovated.

'Ere, Reg, dew ya know wha' happened tew old Sam's boat at all?' asked John.

'No idea … oi've never really thought about it.'

'Tha' don't surproise me,' muttered George under his breath.

'Wha' was tha' …?'

'Nothin' Reg, oi was just thinkin' out loud loike we dew sometoimes,' said George hastily conjuring up a different conversation, 'Oi was jus' troiyin' tew think about an old film they made here … wha' was it called now?'

'Tha's roight … they did, dint they,' replied John thinking hard, 'It had a funny title … err … something breeze … tha's roight, "Ha'penny Breeze".'

'Tha's it – tha' was wha' oi was troiyin' t'think of – "Ha'penny Breeze",' replied George.

'It was a black an' whoite film made in the fifties weren't it,' continued John, 'Yew see tha' big soign over there with Harry King boat builders painted on it, well, the characters in the film were boat builders and they actually used the surname King for the family in it – oi thought oi'd mention tha' tew ya, jus' in case it come up in a pub quiz or somethin'!'

'Oh yeah, yor roight – oi can remember tha' now, John.'

'Lovejoy was filmed here tew, weren't it?' added Reg.

'Yeah, tha's roight Reg, tha's another one,' replied John.'

'Oi loiked Lovejoy, tha' was a really good programme tha,' continued Reg, '... his understudy Eric, took over this pub dint he?'

'Somethin' loike tha' – oi can't really remember wha' he did. Oi can remember him servin' up pints here in the programme, but tha's all,' replied John.

Suddenly, they're distracted by the sound of sawing wood by a man working on a boat. They curiously watch for a while as the man prepared to fit a plank of wood into place.

'Makes ya think, don't it ...?' said John thoughtfully.

'Wassat?' replied George.

'Some of the things tha' must've gone on here in olden toime's, oi mean, it's known tha' smugglin' went on all along this river but it just make ya wonder wha' really must've happened here. If only we could step back in toime and spoiy on the going's on – tha' would be somethin' wouldn't it?'

'Loike a floiy on the wall ...!' piped up Reg. 'Only, we'd hev to hev a toime machine tha' looked loike a floiy ... and all be shrunk down tew the soize of one as well. Tha' would be sloightly tricky t'dew oi think ... just the shrinkin' down bit would be hard enough let alone the toime machine as well!'

'Just a little bit, Reg,' replied John, hoping that the subject would go no further.

30

'Wha's next on the list then, John?' asked George.

John got out the black book once again and began flicking through the pages, 'Well, oi've got an errand t'run later so oi think we'll hev t'make a day of it tomorra if yew two are free?' Both George and Reg nodded in approval.

'Boiy wha' oi can see,' continued John, 'we can hev a look at several places in one sweep. There'll be quoite a bit of droivin', moind yew. If we start at Southwold, then pop into Walberswick, then Dunnidge, then onto Thorpeness, we can finish off with fish an' chips at Olb'ra, p'rhaps – hows tha' sound?'

'Sounds good t'me, John,' replied George licking his lips, 'It'll be worth the droive jus' for the fish an' chips.'

'Tew roight!' added Reg, 'Oi int hed none from there for years.'

'Noine o'clock start?' asked John.

'Foine boiy me,' replied both George and Reg together.

'Okay then, let's drink tew some more happy-huntin' for tomorra.'

Southwold, Here We Come

The next day the lads had set off in good time and rolled into Southwold just a little before ten o'clock. The town is known for its traditional "old world" feel as a seaside town that has hardly changed in decades. With its splendid, white lighthouse dominating the skyline – quaint town centre – fine buildings – long promenade and very interesting pier – Southwold makes it the ideal holiday destination if you want a really quiet, relaxing and laid-back time.

The lads decided to park the car close to the pier as Reg insisted on seeing the very amusing water clock that's placed right in the middle of the boardwalk, 'Come on, quick, it'll soon be ten o'clock, yew'll hev t'wait another hour if ya miss it now!' he cried with excitement as he rushed from the car to the pier.

'Steady on,' replied George with his hand rummaging about in his pocket, 'oi int gotta ticket for the car yit!'

John just laughed, 'He's just loike an eight year old all over agin, int he!'

By the time George and John had sorted out the car park ticket, Reg was already at the water clock waiting with curious holiday makers.

The mechanical water clock is just one of the creations of "Eighties" TV presenters Tim Hunkin, and the late Rex Garrod, who did the series "The secret life of ... the washing machine ... video recorder" and other home appliances, explaining how things worked back then. This particular water clock, standing maybe ten feet high, was constructed from scrap metal and various parts to create a timepiece with some very amusing features. With the continuous sound of trickling water, clunks and rattles, it is a must see for anyone.

George and John arrived just in time to see the clock strike the hour, and with it, join in with the laughter of the happy throng of people who had patiently waited to watch the spectacle.
As the people began to disperse, Reg grinned from ear to ear as he walked over to the lads, 'Brilliant int it!' said an exuberant Reg, 'Oi've seen it quoite a few toimes now and it still makes me laugh.'
'Oi hev tew agree with yew there, Reg,' replied John, 'its loike watchin' repeats of Father Ted on the TV, ya never git bored of watchin' it over and over agin.'
'Would ya loike a cup of tea, John,' George joked in his best Irish accent, 'Oh go on – go on – go on – go on...'
'We shan't say no t'that, shall will we Reg ...?' quickly interrupted John, 'noice of yew tew offer, George. Come on 'en, git ya money out!'
George's face dropped as he realised that John really meant it as he was already making his way to the tea room. Reg quickly followed and grinned like a Cheshire cat as he looked back at George stood there glued to the spot. 'Cheeky sods!' muttered George, but eventually saw the funny side of it.
After their – earlier than expected – cup of tea, the hunt was back on and John had set the plan for them to head in the direction of the Lighthouse as the writings this time involved finding not one, but three lots of dates all to be found in that area of the town.
As they started the uphill walk, John read out a verse: "Up on the clifftop overlookin' the sea, a quiet place for sailors there will certainly be."

'Everywhere here is pretty quoiet,' said George looking all around, 'so tha' don't narrow things down much, dew it?'

'It moight be a graveyard – tha's a quiet place,' said Reg.

'Good thinkin', Reg,' replied John, 'but – one; as far as oi can remember there isn't a graveyard up there, and two; if it was a graveyard oi think it would hev t'be a bit more precoise as there would be so many dates on the gravestones, we'd probably be underground with our own before we found the roight one!'

As they neared the top of the road they came across a small triangular green with a white, boat mast erected in the middle.

'Wha' about here … this is a noice quoiet spot with the mast?' asked George.

'Yeah, it is, but can yew see a date anywhere?' replied John.

After looking closely at the mast and buildings around, there was nothing to be found. 'Let's keep going, lads – oi don't think there's anything about here,' stated John.

They continued the walk uphill where the path then took them along the promenade, and it wasn't too long before they were stood at the front of what they were looking for.

'That's it!' said John with a grin.

'A quiet place,' added George.

Reg then recited aloud the signage, '"Southwold sailors reading room, eighteen sixty four" – it's a library, yew've got t'be quoiet in a library, int ya!'

'Well, this is certainly what we're lookin' for, Reg, but it isn't a library,' replied John. 'It's a museum, but originally this was a place t'keep the loikes of our friend George here under control.'

George gave John a dirty look, 'What d'ya mean; the loikes of me?'

'Only jokin', George – oi only meant it as yew loikin' the beer so much. Ya see, way back then when them fella's weren't out at sea they'd be drinkin' themselves silly in the pubs. This place was to help keep 'em off the beer and do somethin' else better with their toime.'

'If oi couldn't go out drinkin' beer oi'm sure oi could've found somethin' better t'dew than readin' books,' remarked George with a filthy grin and wink of an eye at Reg.

John rolled his eyes and shook his head, 'Come on lads, we'd better move on. From wha' oi saw of the next couple of verses we've got t'foind a butcher's shop next. Oi'm sure the main part of town is down this road here.'

After they made their way along a short distance, they came across the Lord Nelson pub on their right hand side. 'Tha's pretty good tha' int it,' remarked George, 'ya walk less than a hundred yards from the readin' room and ya gotta pub. Oi wonder how many shipmates hed the temptation t'nip down here for a quick pint before nippin' back tew the readin' room agin ...?'

'Probably several if they were anythin' loike yew!' joked John.

'If oi was around back back in those toimes oi could've resisted the temptation,' said Reg, 'oi could give up drink tomorra if oi wanted tew.'

'Oh yeah!' replied George, 'John – its orange an' lemonade for Reg, from now on, okay.'

'Hold yew hard, George. Oi said if oi wanted tew, oi dint say oi was gorn tew. Oi'm just sayin' tha' if oi put moiy moind tew dew somethin' oi can dew it. If it makes a better me, oi can dew it!'

'Wha' about chips?' asked George knowing that Reg was a chipaholic. 'Those lovely, lovely chips all covered in salt an' vinegar, the smell, the texture, the taste, uuum yum yum, the fat, the grease, the unhealthy quantities yew keep eatin' makin' ya fatter all the toime. Could ya give them up tomorra, Reg – could ya?'

'Well ... oi think oi could if oi troiyed.'

'Not a chance mate, we know yew tew well, ya wouldn't last a week – would he, John?'

'Oi hev tew say Reg, oi think George has got ya there. There's more chance of yew marryin' Tess Daly than givin' 'up chips.'

Reg pursed his lips knowing he was beat and looked for an excuse to change the subject, 'Those seagulls are makin' a roight mess on those roofs up there, just look at it all. No wonder there aren't many solar panels about here!'

John and George quietly grinned at one another before John, the peace-keeper, replied in helping Reg move on, 'Yor roight there, Reg. It's a good job those gull's don't grow the soize of cow's, we'd be half afraid t'walk around here if they did.'

'Tew roight,' laughed Reg, as they neared the high street.

'Roight lads, listen up,' said John as he opened up the book. "Bearing two dates, the oldest shop in town; this meat provider celebrates a period of the crown." There's also some smaller wroitin' underneath tha' say's "deduct the smaller number from the larger, t'get the grid number yew need." Tha's interestin'. Now as far as oi can remember there's a butchers shop just round the corner here couz oi've bin in it afore, so oi'm guessin' it's got t'be tha' – but oi could be wrong!'

As they walk into the triangular opening of the town centre, John takes a left and instantly spots the butchers shop, 'There we are; oi was roight!'

'Well, oi can't say oi've noticed tha' afore, and oi've bin here a few toimes in the past,' remarked Reg.

'Oi think tha's loike tha' with a lot a things, Reg,' replied John, 'loike a lot of people, yew only see the things tha' take ya interest ...'

'Loike chip shops!' George joked in a flash, 'Sorry, sorry, oi was only jokin'...'

John gave George a surly look before continuing, '... As oi was a sayin': ya only see the things tha' interest ya but other things just don't register in the ol' noddle. It's loike listenin' t'George sometoimes; it goes in one ear and out the other.'

At that moment George pointed up at a blue clock on the wall of the butchers, 'There it is, John, the "period of the crown" bit we're lookin' for, it's written on tha' clock – it's the Silver Jubilee – nointeen fifty two, tew nointeen seventy seven. Tha's just wha' we want, int it, John?'

'Yeah, it certainly is; yor roight on both counts there, George, well done. Now all oi've got t'dew is tha' little calculation it said. Which is ... seventeen for the first bit a-a-and then ten, fourteen, twenty four minus the seventeen, that should give us seven, boiy roights – yes?'

'If ya say so,' replied George having not attempted the calculation.

'Tha' one was quoite an easy foind,' commented John, 'Let's hope the next one is tew so then we can quickly move on tew Walberswick.'

'Wobbleswick,' blurted Reg.

'Wha's tha' Reg?' asked John as he jotted down the dates.

'Wobbleswick – tha's wha' oi call it sometoimes. Sounds funny don't it ... wobbleswick ... wobbleswick ...'

'Yes, oi think oi hev heard tha' afore,' said John as he looked at George with a roll of his eyes. 'Come on now, let's go foind the Adnams brewery as it seems the loikley place we're gonna foind the next date. Just listen t'this, "Opposite tew one another just near here, one place of worship, the other makes beer" – so it's gotta be the Adnams Beer Company. And oi see just below the verse in smaller wroitin' it says "the number from this foind has to be deducted from the Snape total to give another grid number" – Ol' Sam int makin' this easy for us, is he?'

'Tew roight he int!' replied George. 'Adnams is somewhere near the loighthouse int it?'

'Yeah, oi think it's somewhere pretty close tew it, George.'

'Oi could drink a pint of IPA roight now.'

'Oi bet yew could, but oi think we'd better wait til lunchtoime before we dew any suppin', don't yew?' said John as he briskly walked on.

As they headed for the brewery, George made conversation of the time when he went up the lighthouse with his wife many years ago.

Built in 1887, and standing just over 100ft tall, this standout landmark can be seen for miles around and is today a very popular attraction to the many visitors of the town.

'It don't look tha' hoigh really but ya git some marvellous views up there – yew'd be alroight up there Reg, couz ya enclosed in a little room.'

'No, no, oi still don't think oi could, not even up there.'

'Wha' – ya must've bin up a tall building or a block of flats somewhere surely?'

'Oi hev, but oi couldn't even look out of the winders then. Oi jus' don't loike heights and tha's it, full stop.'

'Oi reckon we oughta git yew up there and help ya overcome ya phobia, don'y yew, John? Oi reckon if he hed ten minutes up there bravin' it he'd feel a whole lot better about it ...'

'No, no, oi don't think so...' said Reg looking fearful.

John could see that Reg was getting flustered, 'Just leave it, George – we're not gonna hev a repeat of yisterdee are we?'

'Well, oi thought it moight help tha's all. If people tackle their phobias gradually and this loighthouse is a good one t'dew it in ...'

'We haven't the toime t'be messin' about up loighthouses t'day, George, even if we dragged Reg up there biting a piece of wood, so oi think yew'd jus' best leave it, okay.'

'Okay, okay – sorry oi mentioned it,' apologised George in half hearted manner, 'Moind yew – even if we hed got him up there he wouldn't hev loiked the comin' down bit if it was busy.'

'How d'ya mean?' asked John cautiously.

'Well – when it's really busy and people are queued all the way up the steps t'the top, there's not enough room for those who's hed a good look around t'walk back down agin so they hev t'go out a soidedoor and sloide down a 100 foot fireman's pole tew the bottom – it's quoite amusing watchin' the grannies come down with their frocks around their earholes.'

'They don't, dew they?' Reg asked in all seriousness.

'Of course they blinkin' don't!' replied John rolling his eyes while George laughed like hiena, 'Oi don't know Reg, yor so gullible at toimes.'

Within moments they arrived at the entrance to the Adnams brewery yard and all eyes were soon scanning the walls and signs for a date.

The site was purchased in 1872 and stands tall and industrial like with some modern structural features having been made to the main entrance within the yard in recent years.

Guided tours are very popular addition to the Adnams beer experience.

'Oi can't for the loife of me see a date anywhere, can yew?' asked George.

'Nope, not a sausage,' replied Reg.

John was still looking up and down but to no avail, 'Oi'd expect us t'struggle after we've hed a few pints but not when we're stone-cold sober. P'rhaps there isn't one here ... wait a minute, we're forgettin' somethin' ... the verse said somethin' about a place of worship.'

They all turned round to look across the road behind them in the expectation of maybe seeing a church tower, but a tree on a small green obscured their view to the wider area.

As they crossed the road with eyes scanning feverishly, they were still struggling until George pointed in the direction of another tree.

'Wha's tha' over there behoind tha' tree ... its a little chapel int it?

As they walked towards it, John leaned his neck to one side to try and get a better view, 'Oi think yew're roight, yeah, oi can see the date from here. Well done, George!'

'Wa-hoo!' cheered Reg, 'Oi'm enjoyin' this. Tha's three lots of dates on the trot an' we int bin here long.'

'Yep, we're dorn alroight' replied John. 'Eighteen thirty foive, tha's quoite an old one ...'

'Tha' was the year yew were born weren't it, Reg?' joked George.

'Thank yew, George – well oi'm pretty sure we'll foind your birth date pretty soon somewhere tew ... in a museum in the fossil collection, most probably.'

'Oooo, listen at him, John. Tha's quick for yew, Reg.'

'Righto, yew two, we're done here so let's git back tew the car pronto and move on t'Walberswick – remember, we're on a mission today t'foind as many dates as we can.'

'Tew true, tew true,' replied George, 'we don't want t'prolong gittin' our hands on wha' goodies is comin' tew us, dew we – we'll jog back shall we?'

'Er ... oi don't think so, George,' replied John, 'unless tha' is of course if ya want t'wake up on the pavement with a crowd around ya!'

'And oi thought Reg was the only gullible one round here,' grinned George with raised eyebrows.

Walberswick

On route to Walberswick, conversation turned to Suffolk Sam, as John was curious to know if Reg knew a lot more about this mysterious man than he previously thought.

"So Reg, this Sam had no family tha' ya know of and no other connections other than the bloke in the pawnbrokers and maybe an odd person here and there at Pin Mill. They're all probably dead now anyway, but isn't there just one person yew can think of *somewhere* that moight know of him?'

'No!' replied Reg bluntly.

'So basically, we int ever gonna know sod all about him then,' remarked George.

'What was his surname?' asked John.

'Err ... Williamson, tha's it, Williamson.'

'Sam Williamson,' repeated John, 'Samuel Williamson ... sounds a good name, sort of important, not ordinary loike moine – John "the has been" Green.'

'He dint speak posh at all 'en, Reg?' asked George.

'Nope, he was just loike one of us – a country boy. But, he used t'be able t'put on different voices loike when he told me stories – he was really funny.'

'He sounds very similar tew tha' TV character, wha's his name now ... err ... Raffles, tha's roight,' commented John. 'He used t'go round nicking stuff from the rich, didn't he? And he could dew the different voices tew ...'

'And disgoiuses,' added George. 'Tha' was a good TV series, tha' was. Anthony Valentoine played the part – he was pretty good weren't he?'

'Yeah, he was indeed,' replied John, deep in thought.

'Wha' ya thinkin'?' asked George, looking across at John.

'Oi was troiyin' t'think what era tha' was in couz there were horses an' carriages he used tew travel about in, so it must've bin the late Victorian toimes. The Raffles books were written somewhere around about tha' toime, oi think, and it just got me thinkin' – '

Before John could say another word, Reg had a thought of his own, 'If Sam was eighty when he doied in noineteen eighty, he must've bin born in noineteen hundred – tha's about tha' toime int it?'

'Ve-e-e-ry good, Reg,' joked George sarcastically, 'ya git a gold sticker for tha'.'

'Well ... you're just about roight there, Reg,' replied John. 'Boiy moiy reckonin', Sam could've been born in eighteen noinety noine if he doied just before his eighty first birthday – but whatever – the books were written about tha' toime and were very popular back then, so, our Samuel may possibly have read one or two and bin influenced boiy them early in his loife, who knows – he may have bin a real loife Raffles, for all we know?'

'But just not a posh one,' remarked George. 'He dint play cricket, did he Reg?'

'Not tha' oi know of ... but he did loike a game of draughts though, we used t'play tha' quoite a lot.'

'*Ummm – it's not quite as dashing a game, is it Reg me old fellow?*' replied George in a well-spoken tone.

Just then, John spotted the village entrance sign up ahead, 'Hey up boys, we're here!'

As they drove into the village the road narrowed and meandered very slightly, where upon, George had to be very wary of coming face to face with oncoming traffic along this sometimes busy, short stretch of road.

Walberswick can be *very busy* in the summer months due to its old world charm, having hardly changed in over a hundred years. It's also a very popular destination thanks to its crabbing events, as the sea at high tide flows into a long, muddy creek that meanders over a large area, where upon families with their buckets and lines can be seen dotted around its edges having fun.

'Wha' are we lookin' for this toime?' asked George.

'Hold on a minute, let me hev a look,' said John as he looked in the book, "Look for a soign tha' holds a period of toime; with help from the village the answer will be thoine."

'Wha's tha' s'posed tew mean?' asked George.

John shook his head, 'Oi'm not really sure. P'rhaps it'll seem obvious when we see it.'

As they approached the main part of the village, the road came to a bend that took a sharp left towards a green that was overlooked by old cottages.

As they drove at a snail-pace, John and George peered out of the car windows looking for the usual signs on cottage end walls or doorways but as the saying goes, sometimes you can't see the woods for the trees.

'There was a date back there,' stated Reg out of the blue, pointing back behind him with his thumb.

'Where?' asked both John and George as the car was brought to a halt.

'On tha' soign yew just passed.'

John and George both peered round and then George slowly reversed the car back past a tall sign.

'On there, see!' said Reg pointing upwards.

'How did oi miss tha'?' said John shaking his head in disbelief. 'It's obvious now int it. Look for a soign with help from the village – the village soign!'

'And there underneath, nioneteen fifty three,' added Reg.

Standing maybe some twelve feet high beside the road, the Walberswick village sign was erected to commemorate the Queen's coronation in 1953, and amongst its very decorative ironwork, a 17th Century man-of-war ship is portrayed in its centre as the village has had a very historical shipbuilding past.

'Well tha' was a quick one,' said George, 'there's no need t'get out of the car is there?' he asked.

'There's no point really,' replied John, 'we moight as well turn around and head straight for Dunnidge, as tha's not tew far away. Well done Reg, tha's saved us a bit of toime.'

George drove on forward past the green and down to the main carpark near the old fishing huts to turn the car round; from there a great view of Southwold can be seen across the lowland on the other side of the River Blythe.

George then spotted an ice cream van, 'Cor … oi don't half fancy a noinety noine.'

'So do oi, George,' replied John, 'but oi think we'd better move on and git one after lunch. Oi tell ya wha', as yew've bin doin' the droivin', oi'll treat ya t'fish an' chips at Dunnidge!'

'Cor, roight on John, tha' sounds good t'me.'

After a slight pause, an "Eer-hum!" came from the back seat and John looked round, 'Oh … and yew tew Reg, oi int forgot about yew, don't yew worry.'

Reg acknowledged John with a big grin, and they then set off the eight or so miles to the Atlantis of Suffolk.

Dunwich

Dunwich (pronounced Dunnidge) was at one time a town of considerable size with a thriving international port, giving it the title of being the capital town of East Anglia. The land that the town once sat upon – that included a few churches – originally reached almost a further one mile out to sea, but due to hundreds of years of erosion from the ever advancing waves, the town gradually disappeared into the sea.

The museum is well worth a visit as it explains the story of the town's demise. With a large model under glass displaying how the town may have looked, it opens your eyes to the realisation of how much of the town has been lost to the sea.

Tales of hearing the sunken church bells ringing on stormy nights will live on forever.

As the lad's drove on towards Dunwich beach, they passed along the one road into what you can barely call a village – just a small number of houses and cottages either side of the road for no more than 300 metres.

About midway to their right they pass the museum converted from a couple of local houses, then onward to the end of the road where The Ship Inn, awaits the thirsty tourists.

Veering round to their left, they made their way to the beach car park where it's overlooked by the Flora Tea Room and large seating area where fish and chips are served all day.

With the car parked up, John recited another verse from the black book, '"Houses and churches tew the sea have fallen in; this one hasn't, so yew can get yor mates orders in."...'

'Moine'll be cod and chips then please John,' replied George in a flash, quickly followed by Reg, '... and plaice and chips for me please.'

'Flippin' heck, yew two – talk about takin' advantage of a situation. Oi was just gorn t'say tha' the rhymin' is a bit unusual 'couz it ends with the same word twoice. Wroiters usually troiy to avoid repeatin' the same word – it seems a little odd or what?'

'Ooh, definitely odd,' replied George in a care-free manner. 'Oi've got two questions to tha' oddity; one: dew it matter? And two: are we gettin' the fish an' chips before we go lookin' for the date or after?'

John rolled his eyes and then purposely decided to make the two of them wait a bit longer for their lunch, 'We'll look for the date first couz after a bellyful of grub we'll probably be three drowsy old gits without a brain betwin us – and besoides, we can hev a look at the grid an' see wha' we've accumulated so far.'

'Fair dews,' replied George as he quickly got out of the car. 'Come on Reg, at the double! Let's get crackin' and foind this date and then the sooner we can be fillin' our necks.'

George and Reg marched off at a fair pace back towards the road while John slowly took his time as he pondered over the verse. Seconds later, he quietly smiled as he realised how simple the verse was to solve.

Up ahead, George and Reg were almost at a cantor. 'Dew ya know wha' ya lookin' for then, George?' asked Reg, hitching up his trousers as he went along.

'How hard can it be, there's hardly anythin' here. Oi reckon its got t'be the museum couz it said somethin' about houses and churches fallin' in the sea – tha's moiy bet!'

As the two neared the museum, a piercing whistle came from the top of the road behind them which automatically made them turn round to see who it was – it was John beckoning them back.

'Wha' dew he want?' George asked with hands on hips.

John pointed to something on his left; then beckoned them once again.

'He must've found the date,' said Reg.

'Well if he hev, chip shop here we come – oi'm starvin'!'

As they approached John, he pointed once more, 'Yew were both in tew much of a hurry,' said John with a big grin, 'yew've just set ya fish an' chips back three minutes.'

'Alroight, alroight – well hev ya got it then? George replied ungraciously.

John pointed again, 'Oi said the two "in's" were odd, and what hev we got here – an inn. Then there was the mates orders – ship mates – and here we hev the Ship Inn.'

'Where's the date, we didn't see anything when we came along here?' asked Reg.

It's up on the end wall there, see – it's quoite a small plaque roight up hoigh!'

'Ahh ... no wonder oi missed it. Oi did see somethin' up there but being so small oi dint really give it a proper look. Ahhh – oi can see the date now, eighteen sixty eight.'

George loudly clapped his hands together and then vigorously rubbed them whilst eyeing up the pub with anticipation, 'Roight lads, tha's tha' sorted – let's go and attack some grub!'

John looked confused, 'Oi thought yew wanted fish an' chips back at the tea room?'

'Oi dew,'

'Well, the way ya were lookin' at this pub oi thought y'wanted t'go in there.'

'Oh oi dew, just not at this moment. Oi'm just thinkin' of afterwards – plannin' ahead.'

'Oh – roight, oi see,' said John shaking his head. 'Well, we better git movin' and see if we can get a seat and then see how much toime we've got afterwards. We've still got a lot t'fit in this afternoon.'

Twenty minutes later the lads are sat at an outside bench overlooking the distant view of Southwold with the lighthouse just visible.

Whilst they ate their fish and chips and watched the day-trippers milling about, Reg was having another of his contemplating moments before stating, 'Whoiy are there so many young fellas with their heads shaved nowadays?'

John and George looked at one another before John responded, 'Well, it could be a number of things, Reg.

'Wha' loike …?'

'Well, ease of maintenance for one; they don't hev to wash their hair or droiy it afterwards …'

'Don't need a comb either …' added George, 'or shampoo.'

'Some of them could be losing their hair and rather than feelin' conscious of them goin' bald in places they'd rather shave it all off so nobody would know.'

'Tha' seems bloomin' daft t'me tha' one, John,' remarked George.

'But its true George, a lot of blokes can't handle losin' their hair.'

'Tha's a thought – losin' ya hair, tha' is – ya wouldn't foind a hair in ya chips if one of these bald blokes served it up, would ya – nor dandruff either, come t'think of it.'

'Oi'd rather not think about tha' now George, not whoile oi'm eatin', thanks.'

'Well anyway,' said Reg, 'another thing oi don't understand is, when it's burnin' hot they never seem t'wear a hat. The same goes when it's freezin' cold – what's the matter with 'em; oi couldn't walk around loike tha'?'
Both John and George turned and wryly looked at Reg who was wearing a floppy hat that had seen better days, having a similar look to a flower after a cloudburst.

'Well, yew know the old sayin', Reg,' grinned George, "Where there's no sense, there's no feelin'."'

After a slight pause and several mouthfuls of chips, John added another theory to Reg's question, '... and another thing is Reg, some blokes think havin' a bald head makes them look sexy and masculine to women –'

'Cods-sthwallop!' loudly remarked George with a mouthful of chips that got the attention of a bald headed man and his wife sat at a nearby table to look round. Having noticed he was overheard, George shrunk his head down low to his plate and with a hushed voice added, 'Any of these fellas who think they look sexy are flippin' deluded, mate.'

John, also speaking in a quieter tone, continued, 'Well, they moight think they're a Bruce Willis or a Jason Statham – although hevin' said tha', Statham int fully bald –'

'Loike oi said – deluded, mate!' said George with a quick glance over at the bald headed man. 'We are havin' a pint at the pub after this int we?" asked George trying to change the subject. John looked at his watch.

'Well, we were quick at Walberswick and here, so oi shouldn't see whoiy not. We'll have another tot up of the dates and words in the pub t'see wha' we've got and then we can move on to Soizewell – tha' int tew far away, okay?' With acknowledged nods of agreement they finished off their meal and made for the pub.

Sizewell

As soon as anyone mentions the name Sizewell, thoughts of the nuclear power stations usually come to the fore. The old decommissioned 'A' plant that started life in 1966, looms large as you arrive at the beach car park. This huge hulk of a building looks sinister and menacing but now sits quietly having ceased working since 2006. The newer looking 'B' plant replacement with its blue cladding and huge white dome can be seen for many miles around and has now been supplying electricity to the area for some 25 years.

Surprisingly, Sizewell is quite a popular destination for day-tripper's and those who use the Beach View Holiday Park, only a stone's throw from the beach. Also, there are some good walks in both directions with the northerly route taking you to the back of the RSPB Minsmere Nature Reserve.

As our trio rolled into the car park, Reg had some reservations about the place, 'Oh this place give me the willies it does!'

'Don't tell me,' mused John, 'yew think we're all gonna glow broight green boiy the toime we leave here later – is tha' it?'

George started to laugh.

'Well ...' squirmed Reg, 'there's all tha' radioactive stuff gorn on in there tha's bad for us, int there?'

'Reg, yew silly old sod,' laughed George, 'If ya sat boiy the reactor maybe, but the whole building is insulated an' mega-safe. Nobody would be allowed to live here if it wasn't safe.'

'There's more radiation hittin' yew from the sun t'day than there is comin' out of tha' place, Reg – honestly,' added John.

'Yew'll hev caught a noice bit of sunshoine boiy the end of t'day, so afore yew go t'bed tonoight, Reg, switch the loight out and then take a look in the mirror for a couple of minutes, yew'll see wha' we mean then,' joked George, trying to look as serious as possible.

'Really – radiation from the sun?' replied Reg looking worried.

'Really …' joked John, playing along with George. 'Anyway – let's forget all about this radiation stuff and get foindin' this next date.'

As George parked the car, John once more searched in the book for the appropriate verse to recite: "A clifftop walk way past the big house on the hill, yew'll foind a date on the drainpoipes, yew honestly will."

'Date on the drainpoipes?' queried George, 'Wha' dew it mean; date on the drainpoipes? Drainpoipes on a house … drainpoipes along the ground … drainpoipes to the sea – oi can't say oi've ever sin any dates on drainpoipes afore?'

'Oi'm not sure either,' replied John with a perplexed look' 'Oi vaguely seem t'think oi hev sin a date on a drainpoipe somewhere before … well, there's only one way t'foind out int there – we'll just hev t'go and see wha's out there!'

'It's your turn for the car park ticket this toime, Reg,' said George as he looked over his shoulder with raised eyebrows in expectancy.

'Oh … oh, alroight, yeah … um …' muttered Reg, as he then struggled to get his hands into his pockets.

'Wouldn't it be easier t'get out of the car first, rather than hev a foight with those draws of yours?' said a bemused George.

After a struggle, Reg seemed to be in trouble, 'Now oi can't get me hands out of me pockets.'

'For goodness sake, he's still got his seat belt on! – John, let him out of the car will ya?'

With a deep sigh, John shook his head and got out of the car. After opening Reg's door, he leaned in to release the seat belt, when suddenly, 'Aarghh ... croikies ... me back has gone ... oi can't move ... arghh! ... arghhh! ...'

George quickly got out of the car and ran round to John's aid and grabbed him by his hips to pull him out. 'GET OFF – GET OFF – DON'T TOUCH ME!' yelled John in agony.

With his head almost touching Reg's, John tried to calm himself, '... Just give me a minute – oi daren't move!' he said with a strained voice, as the scene then began to get strange looks from other people on the car park.

As John was set motionless, George was aware of onlookers and then tried to look inconspicuous by milling around with a quiet whistle and hands in his pockets.

With John and Reg so close together, Reg was almost cross-eyed looking up close, 'Oi never knew yew head such hairy ears, John.'

'Yew what?' asked John as he grimaced in pain.

'Ya earholes ... oi never knew they were so hairy; oi've never noticed afore.'

John was in no condition for such a conversation and was none too pleased, 'Reg – oi'd appreciate it if yew dint analyse moiy body parts at this precoise moment in toime as of roight now moiy fist moight happen tew analyse the end of your snout!' growled John with gritted teeth.

Reg quickly overted his eyes and sat tight-lipped while John then made a tentative effort to take a step backwards out of the car. Whilst making the move, he was sucking in short breaths of air through his tightened lips sounding like a steam train, 'Phw-ooo, phw- ooo ... oi think it's startin' tew ease a bit.'

'Dew ya want any help?' asked George.

'No, oi'll be alroight oi'll get there in a minute – phw-ooo. Go round the othersoide and see if yew can sort Reg out – phw-ooo!'

George went round the car and then proceeded to unclip Reg's seat-belt, 'All we want now is for moiy back t'go as well and it'll look loike someones hevin' a baby in the back here!'

As John gingerly took another step backwards holding on to the door, George released Reg, 'Come on Houdini, yew'd better come out of this soide.'

As George backed out, Reg leaned and fell across the back seat enabling him to remove his hands from his pockets, 'Sorry boys, oi always seem t'hev a habit of makin' loife difficult.'

'We had noticed,' replied George rolling his eyes.

Reg shuffled across the seats, got out of the car and then rummaged once more into his pockets to reveal some coins, 'Ten – twenty – foive and two ... oi've only got twenty seven pee.'

'Yew what?' scornfully answered George. 'After all tha' yew've only got twenty-blinkin'-seven pence in ya pocket and John has gone and crippled himself in the process – oi dont' believe it!'

'Oi'm sorry, boys.'

John could sense that George was about to have an episode and quickly intervened before it went any further, '– Don't worry about it yew two, worse things happen at sea. Reg – come round here a minute oi've ... phw-oo ... wait a minute,' John then eased himself slowly upright with both hands on top of the car door, '– oi've got some change in moiy left pocket ... ow ... phw-oo – hold on a minute, oi'll just grab a hold of it.'

By the time John had fished out some change, George had already gone off and was back with a ticket, 'Here ya go – oi've already got the ticket. Oi didn't want tew hang around another ten minutes to then foind out you hent got enough change either, John – tha' would've done moiy head in after this game of soldiers we've just bin through.'

'Oh – roight,' replied John, 'Well, oi've got some change here, yew moight as well … oo … take some of this – how much was it?'

'Just a quid …!'

'Roight, well, here's a pound coin – go on take it, George – then yew and Reg'll hev t'go and look without me couz oi int gorn anywhere loike this!'

'Dew ya want some help t'sit down?' asked Reg.

'Nah, don't worry about me roight now, oi'll gradually work moiy way into the front seat. Oi'll be alroight – oi think!'

'Where are we lookin' agin?' George asked.

'It said up on the clifftop. Well, there int no cliffs to speak of to the left so yew'll hev t'go tew the roight and hev a look up tha' way.'

With John restricted to the car, George and Reg made their way past the toilet block and round to the right onto an open area of mildly undulating, grass covered shingle and sand. From there they could see a big house up on the hill some quarter of a mile away sat on the grounds of the Beach View Holiday Park.

Working their way along the small tracks through the brush up to the house, Reg noticed the holiday park statics sitting to one side, 'Oi never knew this holiday park was here, did yew George?'

'Nope – oi've never, ever walked in this direction before.'

'Those statics look real noice, they've got a good view out over the beach – oi wouldn't moind sittin' up there with me feet up, lookin' out t'the sea, meself.'

'Oi must admit they dew look noice – a couple of cool pints of beer on the table an' we'd be well away, hey Reg!'

On reaching the large house, they both stopped for a moment and looked it up and down, 'This place looks alroight tew,' said George. 'Oi wouldn't moind stayin' here either.'

As they continued walking along the dirt path, leaving the house, they couldn't help but peer over a hedge at more of the statics and the camping ground beyond which then got Reg reminiscing of past experiences of caravans.

'There's somethin' about being in one of those at night when it hammers down with rain and makin' a roight old din on the roof, and ya laying there in ya bed all cosy loike, feelin' safe and droiy loike a little ol' mouse.'

'Yeah – and those blinkin' magpies wakin' ya up at about foive in the mornin' dancin' about on the roof,' groaned George in his usual dry manner.

'Oi also loiked the smell of the gas fires …'

'The smell of the gas fires?' queried George.

'Yeah – they hev a certain smell when yew loight 'em up, its different tew home. Oh, tha' remoinds me – oi always seemed tew hev trouble loightin' them up – did yew ever hev any trouble loightin' 'em up?'

'Well … there moight hev been the odd occasion, oi s'pose,' answered George, as they began to follow a path into a spinney.

'Oi really dint loike gittin' 'em gorn at all …' continued Reg, 'one toime oi couldn't git one t'loight properly, wha' with the twiddlin' with the knob and troiyin' t'get the ignoighter to work, and when it did, there was a big "woof" roight in me face – oi didn't hev any oiyebrows for near on three weeks after tha'!'

'Tha' doesn't surproise me *at all* with your record, Reg!' replied George with a shake of his head, 'Yor the sort of bloke we hear about on the "News at Ten"...' and then with his best impression of a newsreaders voice continued, 'Today, a large explosion on a holiday campsite at Sizewell, caused an elderly man to have a lucky escape after it had blasted him some 200 metres through the air to land in the sea only yards from the beach. Other than loosing his eyebrows and a few other minor injuries, the holidaymakers on the beach who witnessed the flight and who had pulled the man from the sea, said that although shaken, he was still holding the remains of a matchstick in his fingers at the time.'

'Very funny ...!' said Reg sarcastically as George chuckled away to himself.

As they continued along the footpath, the clifftop walk reached a spinney which then carries on for most of the way along its path. It's an easy, pleasant walk with occasional openings here and there allowing views down onto the beach, with the shady parts most welcome on those really hot days.

George got a little concerned about the distance they were walking, 'How far d'ya reckon we've got t'walk along here 'en, Reg – half a moile, a moile?'

'Well, it can't be tew far ... whatever tha' is we hope t'foind? If we go tew far we'll end up in Thorpeness at this rate!'

A few minutes later, the pathway took a slight downhill with a high wall to their right, and in the distance they could see what looked like a tunnel.

'Wha' hev we got up here then?' said George as he gave a squinted look through the dappled light of the trees.

'Oi dunno,' answered Reg, 'It looks loike a bridge of some sort.'

As they got closer it became clear that it was part of an extension to a large house to their right.

'It looks loike a balcony of some sort to look out over the sea,' said George pointing up, 'oi can see some seats up there.'

'Dew ya reckon there's some poipes under there, George?'

'Oi don't know – its possible oi s'pose.'

As they walked under the concrete construction, the light was poor like the darkness of a tunnel, when suddenly, a young boy of about ten years of age jumped out infront of them from behind a pillar, "BOO!" he yelled out loudly before quickly running off laughing, which made both George and Reg jump with fright …

'*Flamin' parsnips!*' exclaimed George with one hand to his chest, 'Blinkin' humbug, jumpin' out loike tha' – he nearly gave me a heart attack then!' He then turned round to see Reg sitting on the ground, also with one hand to his chest.

'Wha' on earth are ya dorn down there on ya backsoide?' he asked looking puzzled.

Reg, slightly flustered, quickly got to his feet and started brushing down the back of his trousers, 'He froightened the loife out of me tew, ya know – it made me step back roight quick and oi just happened t'stumble over – *little monkey!* Look at the state of me trousers!'

George eyed Reg's trousers up and down and was tempted to say something witty, then thought better of it.

'Well, oi can't see any poipes in here, 'said George, as he walked out of the darkness – then he turned and looked up at the house, 'Well oi'll be blowed!'

'Wha' is it – hev ya found somethin'?'
'Well, oi can't say oi've sin tha' afore – look up there Reg – at the top of the drainpoipes.'

At the top of the drainpipe, just below the main guttering was a box shaped component known as a hopper head. Generally made of plastic, some can be made from cast iron and very decorative too if required – some have dates!

'Well oi never,' said Reg, who was just as surprised as George. '"Noineteen twenty tew" – oi can't say oi've sin tha' afore either.'
'Wha's tha' – dew ya mean the date or the trough thing? *Oi'm only jokin', Reg.* All oi can say is, how many people go walking around lookin' at drainpoipes on houses – oi never hev!'
'Well, at least we've found wha' we were lookin' for, George. Oi s'pose we'd better git back and see how John is gittin' on?'
'Yep – job done. Come on 'en, let's see if he's made it to tha' front seat yet?'

As they walked back into the car park some fifteen minutes later, George from afar spotted John still standing beside the passenger door, 'Blinkin' heck, Reg – he still int got in the car yet!'
'Croikies – he must be bad, we must've bin gone at least half an hour.'
As they walked up to John, he took a step away from the car and stood with his hands on the back of his hips and leaned back slightly to ask, 'Did ya foind the drainpoipes alroight?'

The lads were puzzled by John's sudden appearance of recovery. 'Wha's gorn on here 'en?' asked George. 'Are yew alroight now or wha'?'

'We were expectin' t'see ya stuck in tha' seat,' added Reg.

'No, oi'm not tew bad actually,' replied John. 'When oi troiyed t'get in the car and twisted moiyself round a bit, oi felt somethin' sort of click back in tew place and then the pain started tew ease off almost roight away – it still hurts a fair bit but oi can move about now.'

'Well, the way yew looked earlier we thought yew were gonna be laid up for a week,' remarked George.

'Yew weren't the only one!' happily replied John. 'Anyway – ya still haven't answered moiy question about the drainpoipes.'

'Oh yeah, we found them, even if it was a bit off the beaten track. Someone, mentionin' no names of course, ended up on their backsoide – dint they, Reg?'

'Dare oi ask?' said John curiously.

'Yew jumped just as much as me,' said Reg defensively, pointing a finger at George. 'We were in a tunnel and there was this ...'

'A tunnel ...?' John queried.

'It weren't a tunnel!' interjected George. 'The footpath went under a large balcony type thing tha' was part of this big house in the woods and it was pretty dark ...'

'– and then this boiy jumped out and shouted "BOO" and froightened the loife out of us both. Oi just happened t'stumble backwards a bit and fell over!'

'So yew both hed a bit of fun 'en?' laughed John, which made him flinch and hold his back.

'Oh yeah – great fun,' sarcastically replied Reg.

'So – was the date on these drainpoipes then?' John asked.

'Yep – roight at the very top of the drainpoipes on these box things tha' catch the water just below the gutterin',' explained George with some hand gestering of their shape and size, 'Oi can't say oi've sin any loike them afore, but the date was on *them*.'

'Oh roight,' replied John, 'Oi'm sure oi've sin somethin' loike tha' about somewhere. So wha' was the date then?'

There was a pause as George and Reg looked at one another with perplexed looks, 'D'ya know for the loife of me at this moment, oi can't remember, can yew, Reg?'

'Err – it was ... um ... noineteen twenty eight, weren't it?' replied Reg with uncertainty.

'Tha's it!' said George, 'It was noineteen twenty two, not twenty eight!'

John gave a questionable look, 'Ya now sayin' its noineteen twenty two when ya couldn't remember at all, and Reg says its noineteen twenty eight. Yor talkin' about a difference of six digits here and a different word on the grid – are ya sure it's twenty two?'

'Yeah, it's definitely noineteen twenty two, me brain went blank for a moment, tha's all – oi must be catchin' it off Reg.'

'Blinkin' cheek!' said Reg giving George a scowling look. 'Well oi thought it was twenty eight.'

'Nah, it was definitely twenty two couz at the toime oi thought of the bingo call, "two little ducks, twenty two" – oi just had one of those moments when someone asks ya somethin' on the spot.'

'Well, oi hope ya roight, George,' said John, 'Ya don't want t'be walkin' all the way back t'hev another look dew ya?'

'Nah, yor roight there – but it was definitely twenty two – and tha's moiy final answer!'

'Okay, well let's hope it is!' said John, as he jotted it down in the book.

'Did ya loike me "Who want's t'be a millionaire" bit then lads? "Tha's moiy final answer"…'

'Yeah, oi did notice…' replied John as he continued writing in the book, 'the only thing is, we int got a computer screen to tell us if it is the roight answer or not – so hopefully it is!'

'Its Thorpeness next, int it, John?' asked Reg.

'Yep, tha's roight – the laaaand of make believe.'

'Wha' dew ya mean, the laaaand of make believe?' queried Reg.

'Peter Pan, and Captain Hook and all tha' sort of stuff – J. M. Barrie used tew stay there, dint he.'

'Oi don't know – oi don't know any Barry?'

'Yew must've heard of J. M. Barrie, surely – he wrote the Peter Pan stories!'

'Ooh – roight,' replied Reg with uncertainty.

'Just your sort of place, Reg,' George joked, 'yor in the land of the fairies most of the toime, aren't ya.'

'Thanks!' scowled Reg. 'Yor a mean ol' sod t'me sometoimes, int ya – oi tell yew what; yew'd make a good Captain Hook!'

'Yew int far wrong there, Reg!' agreed John with a wry smile, while George in return gave back a villainous grin of the infamous character in question. With that, John just shook his head and looked to Reg, 'Come on 'en, Reg, lets magic our way onward to our next adventure; with a bit of luck, a crocodile at the meare moight hev George for dinner!'

Yet again for the lads, it was just another leap-frog journey of not much more than ten minutes to reach Thorpeness from Sizewell.

Thorpeness

Thorpeness is quite a unique village, as it's not as old as you may previously have thought. It was an idea of the Ogilvie family who owned the land in the early part of the 1900's to build a holiday village there for the middle upper classes of the day. The writer, J.M. Barrie, was a friend of the Ogilvie's, and would regularly make visits to the village, which was originally named Thorpe, so, inspired by the Peter Pan books written by Barrie, Ogilvie had the idea to create this large water playground for children, which is known as the Meare. Upon it, children could learn to use rowing boats and punts for their enjoyment, and on a point of safety – believe it or not – the Meare was dug out by hand to a depth of no more than three feet, over its entire acreage of water.

Many of the holiday homes were built with a distinct Tudor appearance which gives this village that special charm.

Another feature that adds to this unique village, is an oddity that can be seen above the treetops from well afar – The House in the Clouds. Anyone that pays a visit to Thorpeness should take time out to walk up the lane to this building and see it up close – it is truly a spectacular structure.

As the lads rolled into Thorpeness, a sharp ninety degree bend takes a right towards the Meare, and just yards before the turn a wood pigeon decided to land in the road, right in front of car some seven to eight yards away. 'Get out of it, yew dopey thing!' scowled George as he applied the brakes.

The pigeon was in no hurry to fly away and nonchalantly walked about the road in figures of eight and pecked at whatever it could find.

George drove slowly towards the bird to scare it off but it seemed oblivious to the car, 'Oi'll run the sod over in a minute if it won't shift outta the way!' he scowled.

'Yew can't dew tha', George!' exclaimed Reg, 'Yew'll hev the RSPCA after yew and they'll ... they'll ...'

'Don't yew worry!' replied George sharply, 'oi int really gonna run over it, am oi – unless of course ya fancy pigeon poie for dinner tomorra?'

'There's no need t'keep frettin', Reg,' said John calmly, 'it'll move out of the way eventually.'

Eventually it did, and flew up towards an oncoming car rounding the corner, almost crashing into the windscreen.

'*Stupid thing!*' remarked George as he too rounded the corner,' 'Did ya see tha' ... it must hev a death wish or somethin'? Yew can see whoiy there's so many of them lying dead on the soides of the roads – they must be the dumbest birds on the planet!'

'Unloike the crow,' commented John, 'Ya don't see many of them dead on the roads!'

'Super intelligent is a crow,' added Reg. 'Oi saw a programme on telly about them – they reckon it's the smartest bird on the planet!'

'No – oi can't agree with tha' Reg,' remarked George, 'the smartest bird on the planet has gotta be Carol Vorderman – how she used t'dew them sums on tha' Countdown so quick oi'll never know!'

As they drove on and then rounded the left hand bend at the bottom of the road, John pointed to the Meare, 'Look – there's quoite a few people out there on the boats today, but don't yew get any oideas Reg, we int got any toime for tha' today!'

'Oh, ya int gotta worry about tha', oi git sea sick in the bath let alone on there!'

'Wha' are yew on about Reg? Oi thought yew said tha' yew used t'go on Sam's boat with him up the Orwell.'

'Well oi was alroight back then when oi was younger, but floatin' on water now makes me go all funny – oi int bin the same since oi watched tha' film Jaws.'

Again, John and George looked at one another with that familiar "here we go again" look.

'But yew were young when tha' film came out, Reg – tha' was sometoime back in the mid-seventies!' queried John.

'Oh no – oi dint git t'see it when it first came out; oi dint git t'watch it until maybe ten years later on the telly – cor, it gives me the willies thinkin' about it ...'

'On the telly!' laughed George. 'Heaven knows wha' yew'd a thought of it if ya hed sin it on the big screen at the pictures, croikies! – yew'd probably hev spent half ya toime in the toilets!'

'Well, oi'm glad oi dint – oi'm just not very good with some things.'

'Yew can't help hevin' a nervous disposition can ya Reg?' said John, playfully being sympathetic with him. 'We're all different aren't we? Yew int n'good with scary films and George int n'good with spoiders ...'

'*Hey, hey, hey* – there's no need t'bring tha' up, John,' shuddered George.

'Oi'm only statin' a fact. See Reg – even a hard old sod loike George has got his foibles ...!'

'Foi – what ...?' asked Reg.

'We'll park round the corner shall we?' quickly asked George, purposely diverting the conversation.

'Yeah ... there's usually plenty of room round there,' replied John.

After having parked the car, the lads were all set for the exploration of yet another village, and although they may have visited Thorpeness several other times before in the past with a casual look, it's a different matter when purposely looking for something you may never have noticed on previous occasions.

'How's tha' back of yours, John – are ya gonna be fit enough t'walk round here?' George asked.

'Surproisin'ly good actually, oi think it just must've momentarily clicked out of place and then went back in agin – oi'm sure oi'll be alroight, if oi'm careful.'

'Well, don't dew anythin' silly, John!' said Reg with concern, 'ya don't want t'get stuck in the middle of the road or somethin'!'

'Oi'll be alroight, Reg, don't yew worry about me. So, roight then boys – here we go agin,' said John looking positive as he took out the book. 'Roight, let me see now: "Foind the Crown and it will be very near, a place for the needy will give yew the year." There's also a note underneath statin' tha' the Soizewell date has t'be added to this Thorpeness date tew give a bonus number on the grid, so it sounds pretty important tha' we foind this one.'

'Are we lookin' for a picture of a crown on somethin' or dew it mean a pub?' queried George.

'Oi only know of one pub here,' stated John, 'and tha's The Dolphin, back at the top of the road where we came in, so perhaps there's a crown on a buildin' or somethin' – oi don't know.'

'Where dew we start?' asked Reg.

'Well ...' said John, 'the verse says a place for the needy – wha' sort of needy oi wonder, couz it don't seem tha' koinda place tew hev somewhere for the general needy. We'll just hev t'take a wander about and see wha' we can come up with!'

After a quick look around near the Meare tearooms and boat hire, they then headed in the direction of the beach, passing the eatery called The Kitchen.

From there, they followed the road and took a left up a gentle incline passing the charming Tudor designed dwellings, and then on past the country club to the brow of the hill.

With no joy in finding anything at all, they continued on and downhill to take another left at the bottom which then took them on to the Dolphin Inn.

'We're gittin' nowhere fast this toime!' moaned George. If there was another pub about here called the Crown, we moight be gittin' somewhere – but … oi dunno!'

'Oi've got an oidea,' said John. 'Let's ask someone sittin' over there on those benches at the pub if they know.'

As they strolled over, the eyes of the nearest couple were diverted to the motley trio that were then descending on them, halting their conversation.

'Excuse me for intrudin',' said John politely, 'Yew don't boiy any chance know of any other pubs round here, dew yew – The Crown maybe?'

The man shook his head, 'Sorry mate, we're not from around here so we haven't a clue!'

Just at that moment, an employee from the inn was clearing away some empty glasses from a nearby bench, 'Sorry, I couldn't help overhearing you then, but are you asking about the Crown pub?'

'Yeah, tha's roight,' replied John, 'can ya help us at all?'

'Sure – this was the Crown, it got renamed the Dolphin after it burned down in bad fire in 1995. It got rebuilt in 19 ...97, I think?'

This surprised our trio, as well as the couple sat at the bench.

'Of course!,' replied John, smacking the palm of his hand to his forehead like TV Detective Columbo, 'Oi hed a vague feelin' there was a Crown about here somewhere but wasn't sure whether it was at Ol'bra or not, tha' was wha' oi was thinkin' of – well thanks for tha', mate!'

'No problem –anytime!' said the man and away he went with his tray of glasses.

'Sorry to hev interrupted yew both,' apologised John to the couple.

'That's okay – that was an interesting little story about the pub, so we've all learnt something today – cheers!' said the man raising his glass.

'Well, cheers t'yew tew – and enjoy the rest of your day,' replied John with a salute.

'Oi was loike yew, John,' said George, 'In the back of moiy moind oi hed a feelin' oi should've known, but of course, twenty foive years hev passed on since.'

'Well, we must be pretty near tew wha' we're lookin' for 'en,' said Reg.

As they walked a little further along the road, to their right stood a grand building with an archway in the centre of its tall structure, which soon draws their attention.

'Oi don't believe it!' exclaimed John, as all three could then clearly see what they were looking for. 'How did we miss tha'? – we passed roight boiy it when we drove in!'

Either side of the archway on large plaques were the numbers nineteen on the left, and twenty eight on the right, and just inside the gateway beside the road, a sign – Thorpeness Almshouses.

'Houses for the needy – of course – almshouses!' remarked John, 'But oi must admit oi've never took any notice of tha' afore – it just makes yew realise tha' when yew've walked around these places afore in the past, how oblivious ya are tew all these things!'

'Well, oi can't say oi've ever heard of tha' almshouses word afore!' remarked Reg.

'Well, there ya go then, Reg – this is all a bit of an educated tour for ya isn't it? Oi think tha's whoiy your old friend Sam gave ya the book in the first place – t'get ya out there and t'open up ya oiyes tew new things and learn about the history of our county – only ya just forty years late dorn it!'

George's mind was elsewhere as he stood looking down the road, 'And tew think we walked all the way round the village t'foind somethin' we could've sin from the car!' moaned George. Then, at that moment, a pigeon flew down and landed in the road nearby. 'Of course,' exclaimed George, 'It was tha' stupid thing tha' distracted us, weren't it, blinkin' thing – whoiy yew ...' then ran at the bird shaking his fist, scaring it off, but in doing so he startled some people nearby. With the realisation of how strange he must have looked, he quickly stopped in his tracks and tried to regain his composure, 'Arternuun,' he said with a nod and a short, sharp wave. '... Tha' daft bird ... errr ... attacked me earlier ... oi thought oi'd git me own back on it!' he said, scratching the back of his head with slight embarrassment – and then walked slowly back to the lads.

'Attacked ya!' laughed John, 'was tha' the best yew could come up with – and since when hev pigeons attacked people?'

'Well – tha's all oi could think of, off the top of me head – and anyway, those sea birds, wha'sa names ... Terns; ya see them attack people, John!'

'They can dew – but tha's only when yor walkin' about on their nesting soites. Oi don't think pigeons are quoite the same!'

'Oi got attacked boiy a sea gull once, if yew can remember?' said Reg. 'At Felixstowe, weren't it?'

'Reg – yew weren't being attacked, it just swooped down and nicked a chip out of ya fingers when yew were wavin' it about explainin' somethin' tew us at the toime!' replied John rolling his eyes. 'Come on – let's forget about killer birds for the moment and jot down this date. Are we all happy with noineteen twenty eight?'

George and Reg both looked round at the plaques and nodded with acknowledgement.

'Roight then,' said John looking at his watch, 'It's just gone foive past four – let's head down t'Ol'bra!'

As they walked back towards the meare, they passed a track that led up to the House in the Clouds. 'The House in the Clouds is up tha' track int it?' asked Reg.

'Yep!' answered John, 'It must be the only one in the country loike it, oi would've thought.'

'Yeah, it's a weird buildin' when ya think about it, but oi dew loike it,' remarked George. 'Whoever built it must've hed a strange sense of humour though. Oi reckon it would be noice t'spend a week in there – it's gotta hev some hooly good views of the area from up there!'

'Yeah, oi should say, George,' replied John, 'Oi dint know til the other year tha' its available t'hev holidays in it – so nows ya chance.'

'Really!' replied George with surprise.

'Oi knew it used t'be a water tower,' added Reg.

'Oo ... well done, Reg!' said John putting a smile on Reg's face, 'yew've got a bit of knowledge in tha' noddle of yours 'en ...!'

'*Wha*'! Oi thought everyone knew tha'!' said George in his usual blunt manner, annoying John in the process.

As George was never one to give much praise to anyone – let alone poor old Reg – John thought he'd try and see if he could bring George down a peg or two.

'So, wha' else d'ya know about the house 'en, George?' he asked.

'Well ... it umm ... it's about a hundred foot hoigh.'

'Well, it's not quoite as hoigh as tha'. Oi did read somewhere tha' it's more loike seventy foot – anythin' else yew can tell us?'

'Well ... oi can't remember off hand.'

'Wha' about the doodle bug?' John asked, knowing that if George did know some history about the house he should know about this known fact.

'Doodle bug ...?' he answered with a confused look, 'Second world war, floiyin' bomb – wha's tha' gotta dew with anythin'?'

'Oi would've thought yew'd known about the doodle bug story,' teased John.

George looked flummoxed and just shook his head.

'Well, it so happened, tha' when one flew past the tower durin' the second World War, our boys accidently hit the tower with an anti-aircraft shell and did a fair bit of damage. Funny thing is; there were two ladies livin' down below and they slept roight through it – they never heard a thing! Oi thought yew'd a known about tha', George.'

George just sneered and looked the other way.

'Wha' happened tew the bomb?' asked Reg.

'Well, tha' oi don't know. But wha' oi dew know is, we've all lived in this county for years, and yew two hev probably learned more facts about it today than ya hev in all of ya loifetoime!'

Aldeburgh

Just a little under two miles further down the road from Thorpeness, sits the town of Aldeburgh; once, the home to the World reknown composer, Benjamin Britten. For that single fact alone, the town is very well known for its arts and music festivals which usually run yearly in the month of June.

This attractive town which has kept its old world charm brings back thousands of returning visitors time after time to absorb that seaside town feel.

With an abundance of places to eat and drink and other small shops to explore, Aldeburgh is the ideal place for a relaxing day.

As the lads stood by the parked car and had a brief look out to sea, Reg had another of his questionable thoughts,
'Funny name is Ol'bra,' commented Reg, 'whoiy should it be said with a burra, when it looks loike a berg?'

'Tha's the daft English language for ya,' replied George, 'oi reckon someone out there purposely dreamt up a bunch of names and words just t'confuse us all!'

'Peterborough and Middlesborough are said and spelt properly so whoiy int it said Oldberg … and wha' about Edinburra, tha' should be Edinberg tew?'

'Burra – berg – who gives a monkey's, Reg,' replied George in his usual uptight manner, 'the only berg oi'm interested in roight now is one tha' has an E and an R on the end of it, oi'm feelin' a bit peckish!'

'The English language has hundreds of words spoken in a way tha' don't make any sense …' remarked John.

'A bit loike tha' blinkin' government of ours in the House of Commons ...!' snapped George.

'As oi was a sayin',' continued John, 'the trouble with our language is, Reg, is tha' it's a mix of other languages; a bit of French, a bit of Dutch, Danish all sorts – so words get said differently. Take for example, uum ... err ... garage, tha's a French word. It should be said g'rahhh-j, and some people dew pronounce it tha' way...'

'It's blinkin' garidge t'me!' snapped George again.

'Some moight say it's a colourful language we hev!' continued John, 'just listen tew the way us ol' Suffolk boys talk when we say Ol'bra. We say the ol as in old but hev a silent D, and then the burra as bra – we certainly know how t'shorten words, tha's for sure!'

'Well, oi can't see the point in flappin' ya mouth about more than ya hev tew!' remarked George.

'Ol'bra ... ol'bra ... ol'bra ...' repeated Reg, as he looked skyward contemplating the way the word was being said.

'For goodness sake, Reg, y'look loike a bloomin' goldfish!' remarked John with a shake of his head. 'Come on boys, we've got three dates t'foind here – we int got toime t'stand here lookin' loike goldfish.'

'Where are we headin' off tew first then?' George asked.

'Well, the first verse here seems simple enough, "Once a place of debate, don't give it the boot, use the letter M rather than B, t'help yew foind the loot." So, if ya take the B off the boot and replace it with the M, yew'll hev Moot ... Moot Hall – hev ya got tha' Reg?'

'Oh, oi can't work those things out, oi just int no good with all tha' stuff – tha's whoiy the book was sittin' in moiy bookcase all them years.'

John continued reciting from the book, 'The next one says: "A celebration of twenty foive or fifty years is the name of the hall, the street a crustacean, look on the entrance wall". What d'ya reckon 'en George; any idea?'

George was usually quick off the mark with an answer to make himself sound smarter than Reg, but this time he wasn't overly confident on giving an answer, 'Well … um … the celebration thing sounds like a jubilee, couz the Queen's things are loike twenty foive years and tha', so tha's probably somethin' loike a jubilee hall, which oi've never heard of – yeah … no?'

'Tha's exactly wha' oi came up with,' replied John, 'Oi hev heard of it but oi'm not sure where it is. And the crustacean bit – wha' d'ya reckon tew tha'?'

George looked a bit worried as he did a quick side glance to see that Reg was eagerly waiting for an answer, 'Well … um … crustacean … tha's um … um … is it a special loaf of bread tha' oi've never heard of – tha' would give us baker street then – no?'

Reg stood straight faced as he had no idea either but John couldn't help but laugh, 'Sorry – no George, tha's not a crustacean …'

'It's somethin' in the earth's crust … a fossil – fossil street!' continued George, in the hope of hitting the right answer.

'Whoa, there a minute,' exclaimed John with a chuckle. 'Sorry – no, no, George, it's from the sea – a lobster, a crab, a prawn, shrimp, tha' sort of thing. It's got t'be named after one of those!'

'Ooh … rooight!' replied a sour faced George as he glanced at Reg to see him also chuckling away, 'Oi don't know wha' yor laughin' at – oi bet yew dint know either!'

'It was John's laughin' tha' made me laugh, oi int laughin' at yew!' said Reg with an excuse.

'Never moind boys,' intervened John, 'if everyone knew the answers to everythin' there wouldn't be any point in hevin' a

TV programme called "Who want's tew be a Millionaire", would there?'

'Oi always git the giggles when someone starts laughin',' grinned Reg, 'oi just can't help meself – its conjatious int it!'

'Err – oi think ya mean contagious, Reg!' replied John, seeing George smirk, 'Anyway, let's move on tew the next clue. "The first initial of Len, belongs tew this chap, its half way down the Hoigh Street, a little way back."'

George and Reg remained quiet deciding for the moment that it was best to leave it to John.

'Roight then,' said John as he could see that neither was forthcoming, 'Well, we all know the first letter of Len is L, so all we've got to dew is add it tew the – chap – part, which is ...?'

'L ... Leonard ...?' vaguely replied Reg.

'*Leonard* ... of course it int Leonard ya puddin',' scowled George, 'it's got t'be Chaplin int it – loike Charlie Chaplin?'

'*Well, George* ... tha's pretty good,' said John trying to give some praise but knowing that it wasn't right, 'but oi hev a feelin' if we add the L on to chap, it might be a chapel – we'll hev t'see, oi moight be wrong.'

'Sounds feasible oi s'pose,' admitted George. 'Well, let's git gorn and see who's roight. Where are we startin'?'

'Well, as we're close tew the Moot Hall we'd best start there oi reckon!'

The red bricked, timber framed Moot Hall, stands prominent on the beach side of town, oozing age and character. Several Centuries back it was at one time the town hall that contained small shops on its lower level. Today, this superbly preserved building is the home to the Aldeburgh museum.

Within minutes the lads were approaching the hall where nearby huts on the beach could be seen selling fresh fish and other sea food delicacies.

'Anybody fancy some shrimps?' asked George.

John and Reg shook their heads, 'No, no, not for me thanks!' replied John.

'Nor me, ta!' added Reg.

'Well, oi'm hevin' some, so oi'll grab a pot whoile yew two go look at tha' hall place, okay!'

As John and Reg walked over to the hall, they saw some children playing with toy sailing boats on the nearby model boating pond, 'Oi always wanted one of those when oi was a kid,' commented Reg.

'Yeah – oi've always loiked them tew,' replied John, 'noice and simple, gloiding across the water with the sloightest wind – most kids want things with batteries today.'

As they got closer to the Moot Hall, the wall facing them clearly revealed the date they were looking for.

'Oi can see it John, up there on the sun dial – sixteen fifty. Cor – tha's an old'un.'

'It certainly is Reg, the oldest date we've come across so far. Oi'd better jot tha' down. Tha' was a fairly easy one to foind but the other two oi'm not so sure about!'

While John jotted down the date in the book, Reg casually looked around and saw an elderly gentleman sitting on a bench with a small scruffy dog at his feet and decided to walk over and meet them both, 'Arternuun,' said Reg as he bent down to stroke the dog. 'How dew,' replied the man.

'He's a noice little fella, oi've always loiked these little dogs,' said Reg.

'Yeah, he's a good little boy,' replied the man, 'oi've hed him about eight years now … he loikes everyone bar the postman!' he chuckled.

'Yew sound local?' remarked Reg, rubbing the dog's head.

'Oi certainly am ... lived here all me loife. Oi'm eighty six now and wouldn't want t'live anywhere else.'

As John was in earshot of Reg and the old man, he walked over to join them both, 'Hello,' said John. 'Sorry, but oi couldn't help overhearin' ya conversation just then – yew've lived here all ya loife ya say?'

'Tha's roight; born and bred.'

'So ya must know pretty much all there is tew know about the town then?'

'Well, oi don't know about tha' ... oi know me neighbour's granddaughter is hevin' a fling with the married son of the bank manager's sister who happens t'be the daughter of tha' has-been artist who got sent tew prison recently for fraud!'

Reg's head was in a spin and looked more confused than normal as he looked up at John.

'Well ... tha's interestin',' said John, not quite expecting that kind of an answer, '– but oi was thinkin' more about the, what's where in the town. Dew a Jubilee Hall come t'moind?'

'Oi should think so, oi've been in there enough toimes. Cor, oi've sin some stuff in there over the years. There was a toime oi used t'dance with me woife in there ...' reminisced the old man, then paused for a moment, looked down at the ground and then went deep in thought, 'yeah ... they were great days!'

'Is she ... um ...?' asked John cautiously, 'gone?'

'Oh, yeah ...!' replied the old man with a long pause, 'She hooked off years ago with some toffee nosed bloke with a squinty oiye – oi never did see wha' she saw in him! Still ... it was moiy gain, she could talk the hoind leg off a donkey and her voice was gittin' on me nerves!'

Just then George arrived with his pot of shrimps, '– Anyone want some of me crustaceans?' he asked, grinning with a mouthful of shrimps.

All three shook their heads, 'No thanks,' replied John. 'This koind gentleman here has just informed us tha' there is a Jubilee Hall here, and oi was just about tew ask him the whereabouts of it.'

The old man turned and pointed down the road, 'Whoiy, it's just down there a few hundred yards. If ya keep gorn down Crabbe Street here ...'

'Crabbe Street – this is Crabbe Street?' interrupted Reg.

'Yeah ... tha's roight, Crabbe Street,' continued the old man, giving Reg a serious look. 'If yew go down there it's on the left, ya can't miss it!'

'The street is a crustacean – a crab, George,' remarked Reg with a big smile. The old man looked at him confused then looked up at George.

'We were talkin' about crustaceans earlier,' uncomfortably grinned George. 'Lobsters, shrimps ... crabs ... all those funny ol' critters runnin' about on the bottom of the sea ...'

'We were lookin' for a street with the name of a crustacean, but we didn't know wha' a crustacean was and then when we did, we were gonna look for one and hopefully foind one of them on a road soign, but yew've just told us one tha' oi just noticed yew said!' rambled Reg.

The old man smiled, but still looked slightly confused.

'Well ...!' said John abruptly, feeling slightly embarrassed that that conversation could have gone better. 'Enough of crustaceans, oi think. We'd better be on our way lads, and go foind this hall – its bin really noice talkin' tew yew sir. Oi hope yew enjoy the rest of ya day.'

'See ya doggy!' said Reg, patting the dog on the head.

'Boiye!' waved George with a shrimp still between his finger and thumb – and the lads set off once more.

The old man gave a slight wave and shake of his head as he pondered over the conversation he just had.

'Sometoimes we must look loike them ol' boys off the "Last of the Summer Wine"!' moaned John, '... oi can't take yew two, anywhere!'

'There's nothin' wrong with us!' remarked George, 'We're as normal as anyone else ...'

'*Normal* – oi wouldn't go as far as tew say we we're *normal!*'

'Wha's normal 'en, yew tell me wha's normal?' asked George defiantly.

'Well ... people loike ... Boris ... no, p'raps not, not with a hairstoiyle loike tha' ... um ... what about Fred our butcher, he's ...'

'*Wha' ... Fred ...!*' exclaimed George. 'Anyone tha' goes Morris dancin' int normal in moiy oiyes. Come on, yew can dew better than tha', can't ya, John?'

'Wha' about ... err ... Michael at the pub, he's doesn't dew anythin' out of the ordinary, he's always pleasant and sensible?'

'He's a secret knitter,' grinned George.

'Yew wha' ...?'

'He loves knittin' – clickety-click with the needles,' gestured George with his hands, 'Jan, his missus told me one toime when she got a bit tipsey ... told me never to tell anyone, so keep it t'yaselves or oi moight not see any of her roast taters ever agin, ok?'

'Knittin' ... ya jokin', int ya ...?' sneered Reg.

'Straight up ...!' George replied. 'Now tha's not normal for a bloke now, is it? Come on, John, try agin.'

'Ooo ... oi can't think of anyone off-hand roight now after tha' ...' said John getting slightly ruffled.

'Well, there yew are then ... oi tell ya, yew'll be hard pressed t'foind anyone normal – anywhere.'

John knew he wasn't going to get far arguing the case with George, so decided to let it drop for the time being.

Within minutes they had reached their target.

'Here we are – Jubilee Hall,' said John as he looked up at the building. 'Well, we found tha' quicker than oi thought we were gorn tew, thanks tew the ol' boy back there.'

'There ya are Reg ...' said George pointing at the date, 'tha's another in the bag for ya – eighteen eighty noine. And just loike the picture on tha' bill board there of them rock and rollers – we're a rocking!'

'We sure are!' replied Reg with a quick rock and roll shuffle.

'Steady on Reg,' remarked George taking a step back, 'yew'll be puttin' your back out in a minute with moves loike tha'!'

Amused by Reg's dance, John laughed then looked up at the building, 'Oi don't know ... oi must've passed this building numerous toimes over the years and hev never, ever took any notice of it – even oi'm seein' different things on this trail of yours Reg.'

'Well it's not moiy trail really, is it – it's Sam's? Oi said he was a clever ol' boy.'

'Surely now we must be past the half way mark in foindin' these dates?' asked George, as he finished off the last of the shrimps.

'Oi would've thought so,' replied John as he turned to the book. 'Oi'm sure it's a chapel we've got t'foind next ... then its Snape, Orford ... Woodbridge, Bawdsey ... Felixstowe, plus

Landguard as far as oi can see – so there's still quoite a few t'go!'

'Well then,' said George rubbing his hands together, 'let's go see if we can foind a chapel!'

They continued along the relatively quiet Crabbe Street, until it merged onto the High Street, where the town suddenly became alive with day-trippers visiting the many shops, tearooms, and eating establishments that line either side of the road.

'"Half way down the Hoigh Street; a little way back", it said,' said John as he surveyed the street.

'Does tha' mean tha' we hev t'walk half way down the street, then back a bit. Surely tha' would be a third of the way down, wouldn't it?' asked George.

'And where's half way exactly?' asked Reg. 'The road goes further down the roight than it does down the left …?'

'How d'ya work tha' one out 'en, Reg?' queried George looking confused. 'They ran out of tarmac makin' the left lane, did they?'

'Oi think oi know wha' Reg means,' said John. 'Yew know where the famous fish and chip shop is down the far left –'

'Cor, ya gittin' me hungry agin, John,' interrupted George, 'they've gotta be the best fish an' chips in the country, for sure!'

'Wha' – ya still hungry?' said Reg, '… yew've only just finished eatin' tha' pot of shrimps!'

'Oh, tha' was just a mere snack, Reg. Oi could eat for England oi could!'

'As oi was troiyin' to say –' continued John, 'the fish and chip shop is really the very end of the main street … *whoiy are we botherin' with this? How many chapels can there be in the middle of the street for goodness sake?* Come on – let's just keep walking down in the chip shop direction, we're sure t'foind it!'

As they walked on, they passed many places that offered food or drink, or both, which kept George constantly talkin' about eating, '... oi think oi'd be pushin' it if oi hed fish an' chips agin today. Oi fancy 'em down the road here somethin' rotten, but oi don't think me guts would take tew koindly to it if oi did!'

'Look at ya ...!' frowned John, 'yor loike tha' salivatin' coyote off them roadrunner cartoons – is tha' all yew think about is eatin'?'

'Well, oi just love food, don't oi!'

'And there's nothin' on ya either – oi don't know where ya put it all?'

'Cor – oi've only got t'look at sausage and oi put on foive pounds,' complained Reg shakin' his belly with both hands. 'If oi could git rid of this lot p'raps oi could keep me trousers up better.'

George looked down at Reg's belly, 'All ya need is some extra, extra, hoigh waisted trousers loike tha' Simon Cowell fella wear and hev 'em way up over the top of ya belly; they wouldn't fall down then, would they?' he chuckled.

'Very funny!' sarcastically replied Reg with a false grin.

'Well, If ya hed trousers loike tha', oi hope they'd hev zip floies ...' added John, 'couz if ya hed buttons t'play about with, there would be so many of 'em yew'd be ten minutes gettin' them undone and done up agin each toime, which wouln't be tew good if ya were getting' desperate for a pee!'

George laughed out loud, while Reg had the very slightest grin, not sure whether to laugh or not. 'Yes – very good John,' said Reg. 'Oi can see the funny soide of tha'!'

They had walked on about 200 yards, when John spotted a light blue building over the other side of the road, 'Hold yew hard, boys – oi think tha's it over there!'

They carefully walked between some parked cars and made their way across the road.

'Yor roight, John,' said George, 'it is a chapel – and *it is* set back from the road a bit, tew!'

'Ooh, oi see now,' said Reg thinking about the verse, 'tha's wha' it meant boiy a little way back!'

'Obviously!' replied George.

'Well … *it is obvious* tew us now, now tha' we're standin' here lookin' at it!' replied John, defending Reg's statement.

Above the doorway was a plaque: "Union Chapel, eighteen twenty two," recited George. 'Well, tha's yet another in the bag.'

'Tha's the third an' last one needed here,' said John as he jotted down another date to the collection. 'Oi think we've done rather well today but oi must admit oi'm feelin' a bit knackered roight now, wha' with me back stiffenin' up a bit. Shall we call it a day, boys, and dew some more tomorra?'

'Wha' about gittin' some grub …?' George asked.

'Well, the missus will hev somethin' ready for me later when oi get huum – we'll probably be eatin' out agin tomorra, wont we, tha's if yew two are up for some more?'

'Well, yeah … sure,' replied George thinking hard. 'Oi s'pose me stomach can hold on til oi git huum – oi can quickly rustle up an omelette or somethin'.'

'Yeah, oi'm not dorn anythin' tomorra,' added Reg. 'Oi'm not hungry just yet anyway, so oi'm ok.'

'Roight, so we're all agreed on tha',' said John. 'If we dew as well tomorra as we hev t'day and provoidin' there's no setbacks, oi think there's a good possibility we moight hev enough words on the grid t'figure out the answer t'where the stash is. Whether we'll hev toime t'go foind where it's *supposed* t'be is another matter – we'll hev t'see.'

'Ya really think so, John?' asked Reg excitedly.

'Well, things are lookin' tha' way – we're gittin' through it all fairly.'

George put his hand on Reg's shoulder, 'Reg, me ol' mate,' he said as he sidled up close, 'Ya could be a rich man tomorra; yew'll look after ya ol' mates, won't ya?'

'Wha' d'ya take me for?' Reg replied with a dead-serious look, 'of course oi will. If things work out alroight tomorra oi'll bouy ya tha' burger ya wanted.'

John thought it funny and just grinned at George, but George was slightly lost for words as he wasn't sure whether to react with appreciation or make another of his usual sarcastic remarks, 'Well … um … sounds … good … thanks. Oi'll … look forward tew that.'

Reg smiled, winked at John, and then they began to make their way back to the car.

Snape

The village of Snape is on route back from Aldeburgh to the A12 road, some 6 or 7 miles away, and being in such close proximity, the lads decided take the short detour left to pay the village a quick visit, in the hope of finding another date fast.

'"No smell of malt, just tall buildings of sound; the archway leading in, is where the numbers can be found,"' recited John, 'Tha's got t'be the maltings with the tall buildin's of sound, for sure – music, concerts ... they dew all sorts of things there.'

'Tha's roight, John,' replied George. 'Oi'm sure there's only one archway there ... well, as far as oi can remember. It's the one where ya droive out of the place; y'can see it from the road.'

'That'll be handy if it is – if the date is easy t'foind, we may not hev t'get out of the car.'

Snape Maltings began life beside the River Alde in the 1840's. After 120 years of producing malt, it ceased production and closed its doors in 1965. At around that time, Benjamin Britten had been looking for a large hall for staging concerts, and what better space could be found than in these large empty buildings of the maltings.

Providing superb acoustics, it was converted into the Snape Maltings Concert Hall, which was officially opened by H.R.H. Queen Elizabeth in 1967.

Britten died in 1976, but what he created is now regarded as one of the World's great centres of music.

Other buildings on site have been converted to house an assortment of boutique shops, art galleries, cafes and more for the many day-trippers that visit this extremely popular venue. With walks either side of the River Alde in one of the quietest areas of Suffolk, Snape maltings is well worth a visit.

Within minutes of turning off left, the lads were soon driving over the bridge of the River Alde, and pulling into the entrance of the maltings.

'Oi s'pose we'd better droive in the proper entrance and go round and out, as it looks loike they're now closing up for the day,' said George stretching his neck to look round the corner of the building, 'oi don't want t'be confronted boiy a stream of cars comin' out of the archway when we're troiyin' t'git in.'

They worked their way round past the first car park then along between the large red bricked buildings before taking a right towards the large archway that led back out to the road.

'If only we could go back in toime to the eighteen hundreds and see all this in operation,' commented John as he looked up at the tall building they were about to pass under, 'the smell of the malt, horses and carts, steam trains pulling in to be loaded up, tough ol' workers to-ing and fro-ing about the place … oi don't know wha' the youngsters of today would think of it?'

'Puhh – load of softies, they wouldn't last a mornin', let alone a day,' remarked George dismissively, as he parked the car to one side of the exit.

'Tew trew, George,' replied John. 'Oi'm sure the sacks of grain weighed about the same as a big rugby player, eighteen stuun or thereabouts – can ya imagine shiftin' them about all day on ya back – they must've bin tough ol' boys.'

'Oi hev trouble pickin' up one of them half hundred weight bags of taters, let alone somethin' loike tha',' remarked Reg.

'Half a hundred weight ...! – oi int heard tha' in a whoile,' grinned George. 'Sounds better than tha' ol' *twenty foive kilos* cobblers, don't ya think? Yor still talkin' about four stuun though – just imagine puttin' four o' them bags on ya back at a toime and humpin' them about.'

'Flippin' heck, as much as tha',' replied Reg, 'it's a wonder it dint kill 'em!'

'Probably did, some of 'em,' John replied sympathetically. 'Anyway, we're gittin' a bit soide-tracked here, we're s'posed t'be lookin' at this archway.'

As the car was at a slight angle, John and Reg could turn their heads to their left and see the archway, while George had to get out and stand by his door.

'Well, tha's plain enough t'see,' remarked John.

'"Eighteen fifty noine,"' recited George, 'how many words does tha' give us now, John?'

'Wait a minute – oi'm just jottin' tha' down ... umm ... oi'll hev a look whoile we droive back. Come on 'en, let's make tracks – oi want me dinner.'

Ten minutes later, as they travelled south along the A12 heading home, John was trying to work out the numbers and words from the grid, 'We just got twenty three from tha' last one at Snape, but tha's a duplicate of wha' we got at Dunidge, but oi almost forgot tha' there was a note under the verse tha' says we've got t'take the smallest number from the Southwold dates, which is seventeen – which also happens t'be the same as the Shotley number – away from this Snape number which should give us ... six.'

'Flippin' Nora, John!' exclaimed George, 'oi'm glad yor workin' it out and not me couz ya just completely lost me there.'

'Me tew,' said Reg shaking his head, 'dorn all tha' workin' out would make me head want t'explode.'

John continued piecing all the gathered numbers together and ringed the appropriate numbers on the grid. After a short while he was ready to read out what they had accumulated so far. 'Roight boys – we hev the words – under – the – yule – the Christmas yule tha' is – foind – galore – part – stone – lead – lace – sea and place. Wha' d'ya make of tha' then?'

George and Reg shook their heads.

'Is tha' in any particular order or just wha' ya bundled together?' asked George.

'It's in the order as oi read it through the grid from six, tew thirty eight.'

'One more toime,' asked George with a frown.

'– Under – the – yule – foind – galore – part – stone – lead – lace – sea and place.'

George continued shaking his head, 'Well, it's just a bunch of words tha' don't make any sense at all.'

'Not roight now, it doesn't,' replied John. 'We've still got several more words t'the puzzle t'foind as yet and then maybe, tha's a big maybe, it'll all come clear. Who knows wha' sort of riddle ol' Sam may've set in place at the end of it all – we'll just hev t'wait and see.'

'So wha's the plan for tomorra?' asked Reg.

'Well …' contemplated John, 'we'll go in moiy car tomorra as George has done a lot of droivin' about today – tha's only fair really …'

'Tha's foine boiy me,' remarked George with a smile. Oi can hev tha' extra pint if oi want then, can't oi.'

With that comment half expected, John nodded and grinned, then continued, 'So, oi reckon we best start at Orford, then drop back tew Woodbridge, and finish off the day at Felixstowe. Bawdsey, needs a visit but tha's twenty moiles of droivin' there and back from Woodbridge, so oi think it would be simpler t'go straight round t'Felixstowe Ferry and use the ferry t'pop across – it's only foive minutes down the road if we dew it tha' way.'

Reg leaned forward in his seat, 'Oi int gorn on no ferry!' he stated adamantly, 'ya know wha' oi said about boats earlier!'

'Alroight, alroight, keep ya hair on Reg, oi know tha,' replied John. 'Yew int got t'go wiv us at all. George and oi will go over and yew can sit back and watch the world go boiy in the café or somethin' – it int loike we'd be long.'

'Ohh, roight – well tha's okay 'en,' replied Reg sounding happier. 'Oi moight treat meself tew a scone or somethin' whoile oi'm at it.'

'Of course ya can – ya can savour one in comfort, knowin' tha' the human-dustbin sittin' at the steerin' wheel here won't be troiyin' t'steal it from ya.'

'Oi don' know wha' ya mean?' sarcastically remarked George with a grin.

'Right then, tha's the plan for tomorra, boys,' said John. 'Oi'll see yew Reg, round at moine at noine o'clock agin and then we'll pop round and pick up George on route. Then, it's crossed fingers and hope we stroike lucky, hey!'

Orford

The next day, things didn't start off too smoothly as John had a little mishap in the bathroom which put him behind on time for being ready for nine o'clock. His wife Anne stood at the front door with arms folded, giving Reg a run-down of the morning's events, 'Oi don't know; it was a roight pandemonium here earlier. John dropped the lid off the toothpaste tube and when he bent down t'pick it up his back went agin, no thanks t'yew settin' it off in the car yisterdee. He clenched the tube so hard from the shock of the pain there was toothpaste half way up the wall and over me favourite cactus on the windasill – how oi'm gonna clean tha' off the prickles' oi don't know. And as for the poor ol' cat, well, he got an oiyeful tew and yew can imagine wha' tha' must've felt loike havin' tha' stuff in his oiye, poor ol' thing, he went absolutely crazy. Then it ran into our bedroom knockin' over me tea cup on the bedsoide table onto me noice carpet, oi hed a roight game troiyin' t'grab ahold of him – ya just couldn't hev made it up …!

Reg stood silent half afraid to say anything.

'And there oi am puttin' his socks on for him loike a little child,' she continued, 'Is he gonna rest up for the day? Oh no – he's still gonna force himself t'go gallivantin' out on this woild goose-chase with yew two Herbert's, int he!'

Just then, John slowly appeared at the door looking a little fragile, 'Oi'm alroight, dear, it's eased off agin – if it was *really, really* bad oi wouldn't be daft enough t'risk gorn out agin, would oi?'

'Daft – oi think tha's the appropriate word for all three of ya. Oi can never understand whoiy yew men just never seem t'hev any sense or grow up!'

'Its wha' keep us young, dear…'

'Oh yeah, well it's not showin' from where oi'm standin'!' said Anne, as she looked her husband up and down with a wry grin.

'Anyway,' said John trying to move on, 'It's a known fact tha' it's best t'keep moboile with a bad back, if at all possible, as it loosens it up and prevent it seizing up altogether, so it'll probably be good for it.'

Anne didn't look convinced as John slowly walked out the front door clearly in some discomfort.

'Come on Reg,' said John as they walked towards the car. 'Never get toothpaste on a woman's cactus if ya can help it, as ya can see oi'm gonna be in the doghouse for a little whoile.'

'Wha' was tha'?' sternly asked Anne.

'… We've got t'make … haste, as we're late gittin' round tew George's house – we've kept him waitin' a whoile.'

'Oh …' she replied, not at all convinced that was what she thought she heard the first time.

Once John had struggled, with a bit of grimacing, into the car, he turned and smiled at Anne. 'We should be back by dinner, dear – oi'll see ya later. Boiy the way, wha' hev we got for dinner t'noight?'

Anne playfully put her hand to her chin and paused for a moment, 'Well … it all depends on wha' oi think yew deserve – toothpaste on toast; does tha' sound alroight?' she said with another wry smile.

'Love yew tew, dear!' replied John with a grin as he waved goodbye and pulled the car door closed.

As John turned the key to start the car, Anne disappeared indoors and closed the door behind her; by the time John looked round to wave again, she had already gone. He shook his head and sighed, 'Aahh – the joys of marriage, Reg,' he said with a smile.

'She were none tew happy was she?' remarked Reg. 'Oi can't say oi've ever sin Anne loike tha' afore.'

'Well, tha's couz yew've never bin around when somethin's annoyed her, tha's all – she'll be alroight by the toime we get back. It's very rarely she gits riled up, but if oi dew somethin' silly loike this mornin', I usually go an' hoide up in the shed for a whoile.'

Reg grinned then pondered for a moment, 'Moiy Dad used t'spend a lot of toime in the shed for some reason. Oi can't say me mum and dad really ever argued. Me mum, bless her soul, she was a one she was, she could talk for hours on end about anythin' and everythin'. She could tell some stories tew – we never needed the telly on much when she got gorn,' he remarked with a grin.

As John drove off, he smiled to himself and thought; "Poor ol' sod, no wonder he disappeared into the shed."

'How long d'ya reckon it'll take t'git t'Orford 'en, John?'

'Maybe ... three quarters of an hour. Oi hope George is in a good mood after keepin' him waiting ten minutes, otherwise we moight git a bit of earache off him?'

Within moments they pulled up outside George's cottage to see him stood with a handful of weeds in his hand, 'Wha' toime d'ya call this 'en?' he asked. 'Oi thought oi'd pull up a couple of weeds here and there and ended up dorn half the garden waitin' for ya.'

'Sorry George,' replied John apologetically, 'me back had a dodgy moment agin and tha's put me a bit behoind this mornin', but it shouldn't be a problem – touch wood.'

'Well, jus' hold on a minute, will ya,' said George throwing down the weeds near his front door, 'oi'll jus' rinse me fingers in the water butt.'

After a shake of the fingers and wiping them on his trousers, George then got into the front seat of the car, 'Roighto Captain Kirk, Starship Enterproise ready for another mission is it?' he said with a grin.

'It certainly is,' replied John. 'Reg – can yew set coordinates for Orford on zero, three, seven, four, six, noine, four, one, six, six and loight the touch paper please.'

"Aye, aye, Cap'ain,' laughed Reg as he tapped on the back of George's seat pretending to press buttons.

'Wha' was tha' Anne said earlier, Reg?' asked John grinning, 'somethin' about us blokes not growin' up – oi don't know wha' she's talkin' about dew yew?' he laughed.

George looked puzzled.

'Oi'll tell ya on the way,' smiled John, and off they went.

Although a little later getting away, they still arrived at Orford in good time and were keyed up for what could be a very exciting day of hunting for dates.

Orford is another village that has a remote feel about it, and with it it retains that old world feel. Take away any visible parked cars and you would instantly feel like you had gone back in time over one hundred years or more.

It has a fine castle, although not a large one, as the Keep is all that remains. Way back in time, the outer walls were gradually dismantled and the materials were put to better use in building other properties such as the nearby Sudbourne Hall.

Orford was once a busy port but the "shifting sands of time", or shingle in this case, has placed a large shingle spit of more than a mile between the village and the sea and is known as Orford Ness.

This spit can be viewed from the small quay on the river at the far side of the village, where strange, eerie structures can be seen in the distance that at one time housed secretive military experiments from radar to atomic weapons research.

Today, it sits peacefully as a nature reserve.

When visiting Orford, and heading down the road to the quay, look carefully at the front doorways of the cottages and you'll find that nearly all are of a very low height – proof indeed that when the cottages were built, people of that era were certainly not as tall as people of our generation.

As the lads drove into the village of Orford, they were unsure where to park the car, as they knew it would probably be a quick visit.

'We moight be able t'squeeze in on the market place,' said John, 'we don't really need t'go on the Pay and Display at the castle or down at the quay.'

John drove the car round the parked cars in the market place but there were no empty spaces.

'We'll hev t'take a look down the road tew the quay, sometoimes there's an odd spot on the left soide of the road.'

After negotiating the Z-bend, they didn't have too far to travel before finding a temporary parking spot.

'This'll dew,' said John, and quickly pulled over. 'We should be alroight on the soide here. We don't want t'upset the locals by parkin' where we shouldn't.'

As they got out of the car, George looked around at the array of different houses and then noticed something unusual, 'Well, oi can't say oi've sin tha' afore.'

'Wha's tha' George?' said John.

'The curved end walls on these houses on the left here – all the toimes oi've bin here, oi can't say oi've ever noticed 'em.'

'As oi said tew yew two yisterdee, this little tour is openin' our oiyes tew a whole new world,' commented John. 'Droivin' the car doesn't help couz ya gotta look where ya gorn, so ya miss things, and when ya walk about places with the missus or friends, ya so busy yakkin' all the toime ya don't always see things tha' are roight in front of ya snout – this experience has bin good for me tew, yew know.'

'Oi don't think oi've ever bin here,' remarked Reg.

'Really …?' queried John with surprise.

'No, never – oi'm sure oi hevn't. Oi thought for a moment oi hed, but oi must've got muddled up with somewhere else.'

'Yew git muddled up with wha' day of the week it is, let alone places,' remarked George, rolling his eyes. 'Ya int much better with people either, ya thought Johnny Vegus was Captain Jack Sparra instead of Johnny Depp …'

'No oi dint, oi jus' said the wrong name tha's all tha' was!'

'And then there was –' continued George, before being cut short by John.

'Never moind, we don't want t'go through a list of who was, and who wasn't, roight now, we all hev our moments!' said John trying to end any further bickering. 'Now – let's get back tew the job in hand and hev a look in the book for a minute.'

After flicking through several pages he then found the verses for Orford, 'Here we are – we've got two dates t'foind here. Now listen tew this. The first is: "Where in the market place is there a meeting place for all? Study the facade carefully to see what's spread across the wall." The second one is: "A date can be found at the castle end of town, a rhyming word familiar, a drinkin' house renown."'

'Oi know wha' tha' one is,' said George instantly, 'oi saw it when we lookin' for a parkin' space – it's the Crown pub!' he said excitedly.

'Of course, yew would spot tha' wouldn't ya,' replied John, 'Wha' with yew hevin' a built in pub huntin' radar system. But well spotted anyway.'

'Aye, oi'm loike a bloodhound when it comes to huntin' down a pub,' grinned George, tapping the side of his nose.

'With a nose the soize of yours; yew look loike one an' all!' cheekily remarked Reg, taking both George and John by surprise.

With a stern look and slowed voice, George asked, *'Did oi hear correctly then, John?'*

'Yew did indeed,' replied John, 'but remember George, if yew dish out remarks loike *yew* usually dew t'people then yew can expect a few back from toime t'toime – yes?'

'Oi thought tha' was funny – it's not very often oi can think of somethin' quick enough,' said Reg with a grin.

George looked a bit sour, but somehow managed to control the urge to throw some scorn, 'Well, don't yew make a habit of it. Oi'll let yew off this toime.'

John laughed as he started to make off for market place, 'Yew two – oi dunno. Oi don't know wha' oi'm gonna dew with ya both? – come on, let's go foind these dates.'

As they walked back up the road and approached the left hand bend, John gave out a warning, 'Watch out for cars comin' round the bend just here, there int no footpaths – oi almost got run over here one toime couz some dozey youngster was droivin' round it way tew fast!'

Within a minute or two they stopped and stood just past an old, red telephone kiosk, where upon John fished out the book and recited part of the verse once more, '…"Where in the market place is there a meeting place for all?"'

'Well, it can't be another pub,' remarked George.

'Wha' about a newsagent shop – people meet in them?' added Reg.

'It sounds more loike a village hall to me,' replied John, as they scanned every building in view.

Just then, a lady walked past behind them with a small dog on a lead. Reg, as usual, interested in the dog, turned and said, 'Mornin',' which prompted George and John to do likewise. Then, Reg noticed something unusual outside the doors to the building behind them, 'Wha' are these funny, little pillar things back here?' he asked.

George and John turned round to see two, ornate pillars about five feet high either side of the doors.

'There's another two on the other doors over there,' he added.

'Ooo'werr!' said John with curiosity, 'they're strange little fella's – oi can't say oi've sin anythin' quoite loike them afore?'

'It's almost loike it should be an entrance tew a cinema or a post office, or somethin' – wha' is this place?' questioned George.

John stood back and looked the building up and down, 'Oi don't know?' and then walked further along until he noticed a noticeboard on the wall which he then carefully perused. After a minute or so he came to a conclusion, 'It's the town hall – this has got t'be the place,' he said, as he stepped back into the road to have a better look.

'It was roight behoind us all the toime we stood here,' laughed Reg.

George and Reg joined John in the road and all three stood and looked up at the facade of curved, red, brickwork and centrally placed windows.

'Aaahh – oi can see the date now!' remarked John. 'Look, the numbers are spread out roight across from one soide to the other!'

'Ooo'wah ...!' said George in surprise, 'oi dint notice it roight away.'

"Noineteeeen – 0 – two!" recited Reg with a smile. 'Tha's a good start tew the day.'

'It sure is!' replied John, 'It's quoite a noice buildin' really, if ya also look down the soide by the alley.'

'Oi've just realoised somethin',' said George. 'There's a smoke house down tha' alley, not tew far on the roight. They dew some lovely kippers – and pork and stuff. Oi moight as well git somethin' whoile we're here.'

Reg looked at John and rolled his eyes, 'Is it all he ever thinks about – beer and food?'

'Well, oi s'pose it could be worse,' replied John. 'If he wasn't so old and past it, the opposite sex would be on the list tew ...!'

'Oi, less of the old, and oi int past it either, thank yew very much!' retorted George. 'Oi've still got wha' it takes t'charm the gals when oi want tew – and oi've still got some git up and go left in me tew, which is more than oi can say about yew two!'

'Oi wish oi'd never said anythin' now, Reg,' said John regretfully. 'Come on – before he go chasin' after tha' woman with the dog tha' passed us earlier.'

'What about me kippers?' asked George.

'We've only got t'walk over there tew the pub,' replied John, pointing up the road, 'yew might as well git 'em on the way back ... on second thoughts – no, no, oi'm not droivin' around all day with the smell of kippers in me car, oi've gotta take Anne over tew her sister's t'noight, so oi don't want her givin' me earache over the car smellin' loike a fishmongers – especially after this mornin's little t'dew. Yew'll hev t'get somethin' else less whiffy if ya must get somethin'.'

'Ohhh – oi really fancied some kippers,' replied George dolefully, and then he had another idea. 'Whoiy don't ya bouy some for Anne, then it'll be alroight then, wouldn't it?'

'Well, it would've bin a good idea – if she loiked kippers!' replied John, with a shake of his head.

'Oi've only ever hed kippers once,' said Reg with some uncertainty, 'well – sort of …'

'Wha' d'ya mean, well sort of?' asked George. 'Yew either hev or ya hent!'

'Well, oi did manage a couple of mouthfuls –'

'Ya dint loike 'em?' interrupted George.

'No, it weren't tha'. When oi used t'live at moiy old house, oi got attacked boiy next door's cats when oi sat at the table troiyin' to eat 'em – bloomin' hairy grut things – me arms looked loike oi'd bin through some bramble bushes after troiyin' t'foight 'em off – oi never did git t'finish eatin' the kippers.'

'Wha' were the cats dorn in ya house in the first place?' queried John.

'Oi hed the kitchen door open t'let out the smell, dint oi – they must've got a whiff and come runnin' in.'

'So, yew dint think for the next toime – oi know what oi'll dew, oi'll keep the door closed until after oi've finished eatin' 'em?' quizzed George.

'There's never been a next toime.'

'But yew could've hed a next toime, and enjoyed ya kippers, cat free – yes?' replied George, who was by now starting to get a little aggitated.

'Oh no, there was never gonna be a next toime!'

'Wha' d'ya mean – so ya never gonna troiy and eat some kippers ever again?'

'Nooo, not loikely, the little oi ate weren't tew moiy loikin' anyway – oi'd rather hev a bit of cod, any day.'

George smacked his forehead with frustration, 'Oi think oi'm gonna go doolally, John – ya ask wha' ya thought was a simple question ...'

John shook his head, 'It's a pity yew didn't say yew wanted some pork in the first place, this conversation could've been a lot simpler.'

Reg, just a little bit confused, looked back and forth at John and George, 'Oi loike pork – oi've never hed any trouble with pork,' he said in all seriousness.

'Well, we're glad t'hear it, Reg,' softly replied John with a subtle smile that a vicar would've been proud of. 'Come on, let's hevva look at the Crown up here and see if we can foind this date.'

No more than a hundred yards along the road they approached this fine looking building full of character – a building that should be admired first, before being entered.

'Oh – it happens to be The Crown ... and Castle!' commented John with surprise, 'and very noice tew.'

'Yeah, ya roight there – it's a pity we int nearer to lunch,' remarked George, knowing there would be no time for a taster.

'There's the date!' said Reg, pointing upwards, '"Eighteen seventy noine" – tha's two today already!'

'Yep – we're off tew a flier today,' replied John. 'Let's hope it keeps goin' tha' way. Oi don't know about yew tew, but oi must admit tha' all this is makin' me feel a bit jittery, as we're closin' down on this puzzle fast.'

'Now ya mentioned it, ya got me goin' now,' replied George as he rubbed his hands together once again.

'Oi think oi'm gonna need a Jimmy Riddle,' grinned Reg. 'Where's the loos round here?'

'Thatta way!' pointed John, 'they're down tha' path besoide the town hall. Whoile yew go in there, George can go in the smokehouse and git … whatever – as long as it int somethin' super smelly, and oi'll fill in the blanks in the book, okay boys?'

Ten minutes later, John and Reg were waiting outside the smokehouse, when George appeared with a big smile on his face and a bag held aloft, 'This has got me droolin' already!' he remarked.
'Wha' hev ya got?' asked Reg.
'Oi went for some pulled pork,' replied George. 'Oi've got some lovely pieces in here, oi could've filled a wheelbarra up with all sorts – ya can't git stuff loike this just anywhere.'
'Well … yew could always move out here,' John joked.
'Now there's a thought,' replied George, still grinning from ear to ear.
'Oi've got some interestin' news here for us all regardin' the grid,' said John, as he cautiously looked all around to see that there was no one listening nearby. 'It's startin' t'come t'gether. Oi've just put two more words in and the first bit goes loike this – "under the floor yew'll foind" – tha' sounds real good, don't ya think?'
'Did ya hear tha', Reg …?' said George excitedly, *'under the floor …'* and then his faced dropped with a puzzled look, 'Wha' floor?'
'We don't know tha' yit, dew we?' replied John. 'On the grid there's the words, church – house – boat and shed, in there so it could be either of 'em. When we've got the rest of the dates then hopefully it'll come clear, but oi think it's excoitin' we can see it developin' – tha's whoiy oi thought oi'd mention it!'
'Well, wha' are we waitin' for 'en – lets git gorn?' said George excitedly.

To get back to the car they continued on down the footpath down the alley until they reached a side road, and then took a left that would lead them back to the road where they had parked.

Within five minutes they were back in the car and away.

'Oi tell ya wha', Reg,' said John, 'if ya reckon ya int bin here afore, we'll take a roight here and the road will take us round, roight past the castle – tha' way yew can hev a quick look at it.'

'Oh, thanks – oi'd loike tha'.'

In just a little over a minute, John had momentarily pulled over on the side of the road so Reg could see the castle. 'There ya go, Reg,' said John, 'its quoite smart, int it?'

There was a pause as Reg peered through the car window, 'Is tha' it! – where's the rest of it?'

'Oh, it did used t'be a lot bigger with walls, but over toime the people dismantled them ...' replied John before being interrupted.

'The occupiers couldn't keep up with the rent, could they!' teased George.

John looked at George with a raised eyebrow knowing more was likely to follow.

'Ya sin tha' TV programme "If ya can't pay they'll take it away" int ya – well they were a *very* long toime not payin' up.'

'*Really* – is tha' wha' happened?' replied Reg.

'Of course not, ya daft sod, oi'm pullin' ya leg agin, int oi!' laughed George. 'Come on droiver, tha's enough soight seein' for t'day, we've got some treasure t'foind.'

Woodbridge

At just over ten miles away from Orford, the next stop on the trail for the lads was the market town of Woodbridge that sits on the edge of the River Deben estuary.

Woodbridge is probably best known for having one of the finest tide mills in the country. One of only 23 in the whole of the country, this large timber building with its white cladding is a sight to be seen beside the scenic surroundings of the river.

Walks upstream or downstream from the mill are of easy going, and are well worth the time exploring.

Over the far side of the river and a little beyond the hill in view from the mill, is Sutton Hoo, well known for one of the greatest archaeological finds in Northern Europe. There, deep beneath the sandy soil the burial of an Anglo-Saxon King and his 90 foot long ship were discovered with a huge array of treasures. The on-site Sutton Hoo Visitor Centre reveals the story of this stunning find.

Just a short journey down to Waldringfield you can find boat trips available on the River Deben itself.

As the lads drove towards the town centre, John asked a question, 'Wha's the first thing tha' comes in t'ya head when ya think of Woodbridge?'

'Sittin' down and hevin' a bacon bap near the river,' replied George. 'Oi always hev one whenever oi come here – probably will agin t'day.'

'A bacon bap … not the toide mill 'en?' remarked John in disgust.

'Tha's where oi go t'hev one. Oi sit on a bench and admoire the mill, and the river – have an oice cream tew.'

'Oh – well oi'm glad yew appreciate it – windmills are fairly common but people don't get t'see many mills loike this one here, tha's for sure.'

For a moment the conversation went quiet, when suddenly Reg burst into song, singing "A Windmill in Old Amsterdam", 'Oi saw a mouse – where? – There on the stair – where on the stair? – just there – a little mouse with clogs on, well oi declare, going clip-clippity clop on the stair – oh yeah.'

'Steady on, Reg! For a moment there oi thought we hed Max Bygraves in the back of the car,' joked George then asked, 'Wha' brought all tha' on?'

'It's just a song oi've always loiked,' replied Reg with a beaming smile. 'As we're talkin' about windmills, it made me think of it, tha's all.'

'But we int talkin' about windmills, we're talkin' about toide mills,' remarked George being awkward.

'But John mentioned windmills!'

'Yes, he mentioned windmills but we're not talkin' about windmills –'

'That'll dew, yew tew!' interrupted John, as he gave George a hard stare. 'Sometoimes its loike being back at school, it doesn't seem t'matter how much older we get, some of *us* just don't get any better ...!'

'Don't look at me!' replied George with an innocent look.

'Keep on splittin' hairs ...' muttered John under his breath as he slowed for the traffic lights. 'We moight as well use the car park near the station, it won't take long t'walk up in tew the town from there.'

Less than a quarter of a mile along the road, John took a left into the car park, found a place to park and then switched off the engine. 'Roight, oi'll go get a ticket – oi'll be back in minute.'

As he got out of his seat, there was a slight grimace as his back was still a little tender.

'Ya gonna be alroight with all this walkin' about today, are ya John?' asked Reg.

'Yeah, oi'll be foine, thanks Reg. Oi've just gotta be careful tha's all.'

As John walked off to the ticket machine, Reg started singing the "Windmill in Old Amsterdam" song again, '... Oi saw a mouse – Where? – There on the stair –'

'Ya int gonna start tha' agin, are ya?' George snarled.

'Oi will if oi want tew – it's a noice little song. If ya don't loike it, bung ya ear'oles up. And anyway ... don't yew ever git the urge t'sing anything at anytoime?'

'The only toime ya gonna hear me sing, Reg, is if we git t'foind this treasure – and if we dew, yew'd better hang on t'ya hat!'

When John returned to the car, he gingerly sat down on the front edge of the car seat and placed the ticket on the dashboard while giving George and Reg a serious look, 'Ya behavin' ya'selves 'en?' he asked with some doubt.

'Behavin' ourselves ...?' questioned George, 'we int seven year olds, ya cheeky sod!'

'Well ... oi never know with yew George, being the wind up merchant tha' ya are. Anyway, let's move on and hev a look in the book and see wha's up next.'

As John flicked through the pages of the book, Reg started singing again, 'Oi saw a mouse – where? –'

'*Oh, not again!*' groaned George, as he put his hands to his ears. 'Hurry up John and git readin' the verses and put me out of me misery – please!'

'Here we are ...' grinned John, 'Oi – Pavarotti back there! Just listen up a minute, here's the clues for Woodbridge. "With your back tew the bull, there's three dates tew foind;

tew the roight, tew the left, and the other in front but behoind –"

'Wha' – the other in front but behoind?' repeated George with a confused look.

'Hold on, George, we int finished yet,' said John before continuing. '"A dozen upper windows, a building of red brick; a place tew draw water, look out for Queen Vic." – we'll hev t'think about this one, tha's for sure!'

'Hev we gotta foind a bull in a field somewhere 'en?' asked Reg.

'Of course we int!' exclaimed George. 'It's gotta be the Bull pub in the market place – ya int gonna foind any dates in a field are ya, ya puddin'?'

'Well ya could dew. Me and Sharon Smedworth carved our initials with a date on a tree, years ago!'

'Oi hardly think your ol' mate Sam would use a date on a tree –' when suddenly, George choked off and had a look of horror on his face. 'Oh, tha's a horrible thought …'

'Wha's tha', George?' queried John looking worried.

'Regardless tew wherever we hope t'foind the stash, oi hope he dint bury his stash somewhere near a big tree couz if at sometoime in these last forty years its bin cut down, we'll never, ever git t'foind it!'

John looked at Reg, and could see that he also looked worried, 'Oi … think … its best we just stay positive and hope tha' it all comes good,' said John calmly. 'Admittedly, anythin' could've happened over all these years … but … oi think Sam was a smart enough fella not tew hev buried the goods and would've hed somewhere dry and easily accessible for a regular retrieval of things t'keep him with money in his pocket – how much of it is left, who knows – there moight be lots, there moight be sod all.'

'Yeah – oi'll go with tha'. Oi loike the dry, easily accessible bit; oi think we best stick with tha' thought,' said George, nodding in a positive manner with Reg doing likewise.

'Okay then, onwards and upwards,' grinned John. 'Let's go and see if George is roight about the pub …?'

'Oh, don't yew worry – yew know me – oi know me pubs.'

'Naturally,' replied John whimsically, with a winked eye at Reg.

They made their way from the car park, past the station and then over the road to Quay Street, where they then followed it up the quarter of a mile or so, to the market square.

'The Bull is just on the roight here,' said George pointing a finger.

'Do ya see somethin' else on our left as well?' hinted John.

'It's Queen Victoria,' stated Reg, 'is tha' the Queen Vic we're lookin' for?'

A wartime memorial garden is situated to their left with a large cross centrally placed within it, and not too far away to one side stood a statue of Queen Victoria on a plinth.

'Roight then, Mister pub expert – just to be sure tha' we've got the roight Queen Vic, is there a Victoria pub anywhere near here?' asked John.

'No – oi'm pretty sure there int no such pub anywhere around here.'

'Well Reg, as yew can see there's a date down there on the plinth, oi'd say tha's *exactly* wha' we're lookin' for.'

"Eighteen eighty seven," recited Reg, then he queried the date. 'Oi thought she died in noineteen hundred and somethin'?'

'Noineteen o one, weren't it, John?' stated George.

'Yeah, ya roight George, it was noineteen o one, but eighteen eighty seven don't mean anything' tew me, oi int gotta clue ... oh, wait a minute ... if she came tew the throne in thirty seven and tha's eighty seven on there, tha's fifty years innit – so tha's gotta be the year of her silver ... *no, oi mean,* golden jubilee.'

Reg was impressed, 'Cor – yew soon figured tha' out John. Whoiy can't oi be clever loike yew sometoimes?' he asked.

'Couz yew most probably were somewhere near the back of the queue when they handed out the brains ...' joked George.

'Now, now, George ...!' said John in Reg's defence. 'If there were brains graded from one to ten – noice to mean – yours would definitely be somewhere around eight, so tha' wouldn't be somethin' t'be proud of, would it?'

'Oh, come on! Yew make me sound loike oi'm *really* mean. Oi just loike a joke.'

'We all like a joke,' replied John, 'but not always at someone else's expense – yew just can't see it, can ya?'

George looked skyward, 'Err – no, oi don't,' he answered with an innocent grin.

John shook his head, 'Oi don't suppose yew'll ever change will ya, not for a moment?'

'Oi don't know wha' your gorn on about, there's nothin' t'change. Oi'm just loike everyone else – well, not quoite loike Reg, but...'

John knew he wasn't getting through to him and started to walk towards the Bull Inn, 'Oi don't know, Reg, wha' are we gonna dew with him? Come on; let's look for some more dates.'

The three of them wandered over to the Bull Inn and then stood together side by side on the edge of the pavement with their backs to the pub.

'Roight then,' said John, 'oi've jotted tha' date down, "eighteen eighty seven", and now we've got t'look somewhere tew our roight: "A dozen upper windows, a buildin' of red brick" it says ...'

'There!' pointed George. 'Oi think oi can see a plaque up on tha' wall up there,' and then proceeded to cross the road.

'Hold yew hard a minute!' said John sternly. 'Oi int finished yet! We can all go an' hev a look after oi've read the next bit couz we moight need t'stand here t'make any sense of it, roight? So listen up: "Tew the roight ... tew the left, and the other in front but behoind" and, it also says, "go draw some water", so wha' hev we got?'

'We've got a pub behoind us, they'd hev water,' commented Reg.

'Not in the beer, oi hope,' said George with a grin.

'So wha' hev we got in front of us ...?' asked John, 'The town hall is the only building sat roight in the middle of the market place. Perhaps there's a date on the back of it – *in front but behoind*?'

Well there's only one way t'foind out, int there,' as George marched off once again.

They all crossed the road with George striding out several yards ahead like he was on a mission, "Eighteen sixty!" he recited loudly, before John and Reg could get up close.

"A dozen upper windows," recited Reg, as he looked up counting them with his finger.

'We already know tha'!' remarked George in his usual surly manner, 'The date is roight there in front of ya!'

John said nothing but looked at George with raised eyebrows and a questionable look.

'Alroight, alroight – oi git the message!' said George with a half-hearted apology.

John opened the black book and jotted down the date and then turned and looked at the town hall, 'Tha's an unusual buildin' with those steps up t'that door,' he remarked. 'Oi assume there's no internal stairs by the look of it?'

'Well, if tha's the case, it's not so good if the toilet is downstairs and it's chuckin' it down with rain on a freezin' cold day – tha' would be a roight pain, wouldn't it?' grinned George.

'It's still a smart buildin' though,' remarked Reg.

'It certainly is, Reg.' replied John. 'Oi'm surprised there isn't a date on the front somewhere. Can either of yew see one, couz oi can't?'

They all wandered around the front of the building looking it up and down, but neither of them could find a date.

'Let's take a look round the back, maybe there's somethin' there?' commented John.

On reaching the back of the hall, a small, but very elaborate structure of brick and stone of approximately 12 feet in height stood before them, 'Wha's this 'en?' asked George.

'Oi'm not sure?' replied John, 'Oi've passed it plenty of toimes in the car in the past but oi can't say oi've hed a really good look at it afore.'

As they studied it more, it then came apparent what it was.

'Oh, oi can see wha' it is now …' stated John.

'And so can oi now, seein' tha' wheel and poipe in there …' replied George.

"It's a water pump!" they both said together.

'Well oi never!' said John, 'oi've never sin anythin' quoite as elaborate as this afore for drawin' water – it's quoite somethin' really.'

'Tha's Suffolk Sam, for ya!' beamed Reg. 'He certainly hed an oiye for tha' arky … ya know, stuff.'

'Achitecture, Reg – architecture,' softly replied John.

'Is there a date on it?' asked George as he walked round it.

'Oh, here it is, it's on the soide here – "eighteen seventy six", tha's wha' we're lookin' for, int it boys?'

'Well, this is the "draw some water" part from the verse, so yes; we've ticked all the boxes agin, boys!'

George rubbed his hands together once again before slapping Reg on the upper arm with excitement, 'We're gittin' there, boy …' he smiled, 'we're gittin' there!'

'Well then, we'd better make our way back to the car,' said John, as he jotted down yet another date.

'And foind some grub tew, couz oi'm flippin' starving.' added George holding his stomach with one hand.

'Me tew …' said Reg. 'Oi fancy one of them bacon baps yew spuuk about earlier.'

'Well, let me lead the way, me ol' friend …' grinned George with eyes agape, 'the pleasure is gonna be *aaall* moine.'

On returning back to the grounds of the station car park, they made their way round to the quay, where stood the Caravan Café, a small, but very popular eatery for meals inside or outside, that has seating overlooking the moored boats.

In no time at all, our hungry trio were soon armed with bacon baps and cups of tea, and with the weather fine with clear blue skies and no wind, the river looked glorious.

'Come on …' said George, 'let's go sit near that shelter by the river; we can see the mill from there.'

Once seated, they could view the mill in all its glory, the brilliant white boards dazzling in the bright sunshine.

'Oi never git bored lookin' at tha' soight,' said George, 'oi've bin here dozens of toimes and oi still marvel at the soize and condition of tha' mill. Oi'm not into buildin's and all tha' stuff but for some reason tha' does somethin' for me.'

'Oi know wha' ya mean, George.' added John. 'Oi can't imagine many folk not being awestruck by the whole setting of it standin' there – especially on a day loike this.'

'Und wiv the hoigh twoide two!' mumbled Reg, with a big mouthful of bacon roll.

'Wha' was tha'?' cringed John, as he watched Reg chomping away for a few seconds more before gulping down the large mouthful like a heron swallowing a large fish.

'*And with a hoigh toide tew,* oi said – it looks real noice with all the water so still, loike a mill pool – ha – oi just said mill pool dint oi? It is a mill, but we int gotta pool in front of us, couz tha's behoind the back of it, but oi said mill pool couz tha's wha' folk say, don't they?'

'Yes, yes, we know wha' ya mean, Reg!' nodded John. 'Oi agree, it does add to the peace and tranquillity of the scene before us – *it is definitely special.*'

As they sat eating and took in the views of the river, John pondered for a while as he stared long and hard at the waters downstream, 'Oi can almost imagine ol' Suffolk Sam chuggin' up this river on a moonlit night. The waters calm as it is now ... the wake of his boat ripplin' and twinklin' in the loight of the moon ... a gentle mist in the distance ... an owl hootin' in the woods ...'

'Oi could do with a bit more sauce on me bacon!' interrupted George, killing the atmosphere of John's imaginative thoughts in one fell swoop.

John gently shook his head and then took a sip of tea, 'It's a real noice cup of tea this – just how oi loike it,' he remarked. 'There's another tea room down the path there, The Tea Hut it's called, int it?'

'Yeah, it is,' replied George, 'oi go in there sometoimes when oi've come back from a walk along the river bank – they make a noice cup of tea there tew.'

'Makin' a cup of tea can be annoyin' sometoimes, don't ya think?' asked Reg out of the blue.

With dead-pan faces, George and John looked round at Reg, with the knowing feeling that a daft statement was imminent.

'Oi hate it when ya accidently hit the tea bag on the soide of the cup, and a dribble of tea runs down the soide and then leaves a wet, brown tea ring on ya worktop – don't you?'

'Yeah – we all do tha' from toime t'toime,' replied John unenthusiastically. 'Not noticin' it roight away and lettin' it droiy is the annoyin' part, especially when it comes t'troiyin' t'clean it off later and yew can hardly shift it.'

'Oi know wha' ya mean ...' said Reg, 'moiy worktop must hev about fifty rings still on it oi can't shift – its tha' bad it looks loike one of them messy works of art!'

'Wha' – flippin' heck, Reg!' said John in disgust. 'If ya do it tha' often whoiy don't ya sit ya cup on some ol' coaster or somethin', instead of messin' up ya worktop ...?'

'Or better still ...' said George, 'drink coffee!'

'Oh, oi'm not a coffee drinker, George – but tha's a good oidea of yours John, oi'll hev t'dew tha'!'

John and George looked at one another and just shook their heads in disbelief.

'Okay then,' said John, 'are we all ready for the off agin, boys?'

'Yep!' replied George as he flicked out the dregs from his cup. 'All topped up and rarin' t'go. Oi think oi'll wait and hev an oice cream when we git tew Felixstowe – if possible, an extra large, double coned one.'

'Well, oi think its best we go t'Bawdsey first,' said John. 'We could drive direct, back along past Sutton Hoo, but as oi said yesterday, we'll go t'Felixstowe Ferry instead. Are yew ready Reg?'

'Yep – but remember, oi int gorn on no ferry moind ...'
'Oi int forgotten, Reg!' replied John with a grin. And they all made their way back to the car for the next part of the trail.

Felixstowe Ferry and Bawdsey

Felixstowe Ferry, as it is called, is a small hamlet just a mile north of the town of Felixstowe. It is yet again another timeless, quiet world of tranquillity placed right at the mouth of the River Deben. And yes, it does have a ferry – a small boat that can regularly carry up to around 15 to 20 passengers at a time from April to October.

After a drive by car or a ride by motorbike with the road at its end, the Ferry Café and the Ferry Boat Inn are always very popular for those in need of somewhere relaxing to stop.

Over the river is Bawdsey Quay, another much unchanged hamlet with very few buildings along the short stretch of road alongside the river. Look out for the Boathouse Café, for a scenic view of the river while you have your tea and cakes.

Just beyond, is Bawdsey Manor, a magnificent building that can be viewed by taking just a short walk down either side of the river mouth to the sea.

In 1937 it was sold to the air ministry where research created the invention of radar. Just a short distance up the road a museum can be found at the transmitter block where you can find out all about the story of the top secret work that went on there that was so crucial to Britain winning the Battle of Britain.

A mile or so before reaching Felixstowe Ferry, the lads followed the road through the middle of the links golf course, which then reminded John of a near miss he once had, 'Yew'd better moind ya'selves, boys, we're a moving target here – get the tin hats out!'

'Git the tin hats out?' queried Reg.

'Oi'm just messin' about, Reg. It just remoinded me of a toime when me and the missus were droivin' past the golf course at Thetford, years ago, when a golf ball came boundin' down the road towards us in really big bounces – fortunately it bounced roight over the top of the car. We were lucky it dint hit the windscreen!'

'Well oi think we're fairly safe here,' commented George, 'they hev nets up at the dodgy spots, but ya gotta be a really rubbish golfer if ya git a ball on the road near them – moind yew, if they're anything loike Reg, anythin's possible!'

Reg didn't respond as he was only half listening – another thought was on his mind, as he slowly said, 'Oi *vaguely* remember a school mate of moine swallowin' a golf ball ...'

'*Swallowed a golf ball!*' exclaimed George in disbelief.

'Yeah, tha's roight, Nobby Sturgeon was his name, he showed it tew me and me mates with it wedged in his teeth, and when he sucked it back in his mouth, he accidently swallowed it ... oh ... wait a minute ... no ... no, it weren't a golf ball, it was a gobstopper ... tha's roight, it was a gobstopper!'

'Oi was gonna say, yew hed us goin' there,' said George. 'But even so, a gobstopper would take some swallowin'!'

'Sorry – oi'd got visions of this whoite ball in his mouth but it goes whoite after ya suck the outer colour off it, doesn't it? Oi can still see it now, the lump gorn slowly down his throat – he reckoned it was pretty painful.'

'Oi'm not surproised,' remarked John. 'It's bad enough when ya bolt some food, let alone a gobstopper.'

After a few twists and turns on the road, John pulled in and parked the car at the Ferry Cafe, just yards from the river. Several wooden huts, boatsheds and boats sprawl out close by with a large array of yacht's and other vessels moored out on the river, making for a splendid scene of water borne life.

'Well, here we go agin,' said John as he steadily climbed out of the car. 'So we can't persuade ya t'come for a boat roide then, Reg?'

'Nope!' replied Reg with sure-fire certainty. 'Oi'll just pop in the café and git a KitKat or somethin' and hev a wander about if ya don't moind.'

'Okey dokey then, if ya happy enough – come on George, we'd better get t'the jetty and see what the ferry is dorn.'

'Aye, aye, Captain!' voiced George in a pirate tone with a squinted eye. 'Me cutlass be ready for action, oi can smell gold a-driftin' across the depths from here – oo-arghh!'

'Very dramatic,' said John as he looked around hoping there was no one in earshot. 'If ya hev a spell loike tha' on the ferry, oi'm not with ya, okay?'

George grinned with his usual look of devilishness that often made John feel uneasy, 'Oi'll troiy me best t'behave, Captain,' he said with a wink and another "Oo-arghh."

John looked at Reg and rolled his eyes, 'Are ya gonna come along and see me and Long John Silver off – we shouldn't be tew long?'

'Okay,' replied Reg.

The lads then made their way down the road the short distance to the ferry jetty to see that the ferry was just then taking on passengers, 'Ooo, we've toimed this well, George,' said John. 'We'll see ya shortly, Reg!'

The two boarded the boat with five other passengers and two dogs, and was quickly away across the relatively fast flowing waters as the toide was on the ebb.

Two minutes later, the lads were across the river and out of the ferry, and from there, they then made their way through some parked cars over to the entrance of Bawdsey Manor.

'Righto George, listen up agin: "Close tew the ferry are some lodges near a gate," – well, oi can see some lodges, but oi can't see a gate – "opposite tew east is the one with a date", so it's gotta be these lodges here on our roight couz they're int any lodges on our left.'

They walked slowly to their right and peered over at the nearest lodge, scouring the brick walls for signs of a date. 'There!' pointed George. 'Opposite tew east is west – it says West Gate Lodge on that sign there!'

'Yep – ya roight, this is the lodge alroight – but can ya see a date anywhere?'

John walked back to his left as George worked his way to his right, both hoping that the date would be on an end wall.

'Oi've got it!' called out George. 'It's on this end – it says noineteen hundred.'

John wandered over to George to have a look for himself, 'Marvellous, George, oi thought for a moment we weren't gonna foind anythin'. Tha's the first round number we've come across so far!'

'Tha' add's up t'ten, so tha's got t'be a real early word on the grid 'en,' remarked George.

'Let me hev a look,' said John as he searched the book for the grid. 'Let me see now ... we hed "under the floor" earlier ... and ... now, we hev the word "boat" ... and it reads, "Under the boat floor" ...'

'Under the boat floor – *wha' Sam's boat?*' queried George looking anxious.

'Oi don't know, George. If ya thinkin' wha' oi'm thinkin' ... it could be a bit of a problem, if it is?'

In frustration, George walked a tight circle with hands clasped on top of his head to groan, 'This is forty, flippin' years on, wha' chance hev we got of foindin' his boat? It moight've sunk or rotted away or whatever ... oi just don't believe it!'

'Uumm, this is not good, oi don' know what t'think roight now, Reg,' pondered John. 'We better get back over t'Reg and break the news tew him tha' there's the possibly it could be the end of the road.'

For the first time in the last three days, the ever confident John felt a little anxious knowing that *if* it was Sam's boat they needed to find, it was going to be a near impossibility.

With forlorn faces they made their way back to the ferry jetty, and then sat quietly for a while as they waited for the return ferry.

John, deep in thought, stared at the scattering of moored boats bobbing up and down on the far side of the river, then stated, 'Even if the boat existed for several more years and belonged to a fresh owner, oi'm sure they would've looked under the floorin' t'get at the engine at some stage.'

'Cor – and wha' a thought of someone foindin' a stash of stuff they dint even know was there,' replied George shaking his head. 'It doesn't bear thinkin'about!'

With the gentle chugging sound of the ferryboat motor getting louder as it neared; the ferry then arrived at the jetty with a burst of revs as reverse gear was engaged to slow it down, and once tethered, the passengers climbed out of the boat like drunkards, as it gently rocked against the siding.

Within minutes, John and George were back on the other side of the river and could see Reg sat at a picnic bench finishing off the last few bites of an ice cream cone, 'Hey up!' he shouted, 'How'd ya git on?'

The pair made a glum, glance at one another as they walked forward, neither one to keen on being a bearer of bad news. Once at the bench, the lads each climbed into the seating and rested their elbows on the table top with hands clenched together.

'Well, Reg ...' said John, with another quick glance at George, 'there moight be a bit of a problem.'

'A problem?' replied Reg, wiping the remnants of ice cream from his bottom lip with the back of his hand, 'Wha' sort of a problem – couldn't ya foind the date?'

'Oh, we found the date alroight, but um ... the word it created on the grid has put the cat among the pigeon's, so tew speak.'

'Wha' word is tha' then, surely it can't be tha' bad can it?

'It said boat ...' added George, 'under the bloomin' boat floor!'

'Under the boat floor ... the treasure ... tha's good int it?'

'Tha's the problem,' said John. 'If it is Sam's boat we need t'foind, wha' chance hev we got of foindin' it forty years on – unless yew know something we don't?'

'Oh ...' said Reg, with a blank expression that seemed to last some while.

'Hello – Reg. Are ya in there?' asked John, as he tapped on the table top.

'No ...' replied Reg, looking somewhat vague.

'No – no wha'? No, ya not in there, or no, ya don't know?'

'No – no, oi don't know,' replied Reg, as he snapped back into life. 'Oi was troiyin' t'think when oi last saw it, but no, oi've got no idea oi'm afraid, boys.'

'Well, tha's it then, int it?' groaned George, shaking his head.

All three sat for a while with quiet thoughts as they watched the comings and goings of people around them, when John then came up with a suggestion, 'Let's carry on with the search for the dates ... finish off the grid t'see wha' the final message actually says – even though it looks loike a lost cause – couz oi think we should still finish it in honour of all the effort tha' Sam went tew in makin' this treasure trail; he certainly believed in makin' the searcher work for the proize, and also, openin' their oiyes in the process. Oi think we've all learnt somethin' good from these last few days, even if we don't foind the gold at the end of the rainbow.'

Reg and George gently nodded their heads in agreement.

'Well, we've come this far …' said George as he began to extract himself from the bench, 'so let's git gorn and finish this!'

John and Reg followed suit, and they all made their way back to the car.

Felixstowe

Less than ten minutes later, our slightly detuned trio pulled into Sea Road, on the southern side of town, not too far away from the Felixstowe pier.

Along this road, to the right of the pier, is the main area for fun attractions, arcades, crazy golf, boating ponds, play areas and the like for all the family, not forgetting, places to enjoy the pleasures of eating fish and chips, ice creams and ice lollies.

To the left of the pier, a walk along the promenade takes visitors in the direction of the seafront gardens that are laid out along the cliffs. With the many fine, period buildings along this stretch and with the restored gardens covering quite some distance, it's easy to see how it was such a popular destination back in the late Victorian times and early part of 20th century when tourism was in its infancy.

'Hey up, tha's handy!' said John, as a car pulled out and away from a parking space on the side of the road. 'Tha' worked out noicely, we'll just slot in there.'

No sooner had John finished parking the car and switched off the engine, George was out of the car like a greyhound out of the traps.

'Whoa, hold on a minute, George, wha's the flippin' hurry?' exclaimed John.

'Oi'm gaspin' for me oice cream; Reg has had his!'

'Just hold yew hard a minute, there's plenty of toime for oice creams. Oi just want t'read out the verses before we go wanderin' off, okay?'

'Can't ya dew it on the way?'

'Oi'd rather dew it here. There's a lot more people millin' about this area and oi don't really want t'be readin' out loud from a book amongst 'em all – just sit down a minute!'

'Well … if oi must!' muttered George, rolling his eyes before getting back in the car.

'This won't take a minute. Now listen up, we've got a couple here t'foind; one's a normal length verse, the other is quoite a long one: "Overlookin' the gardens, it's now called a house, once a grand hotel, now has a name of a mouse"…'

'Jerry Hall!' blurted out Reg, trying his best to be helpful.

'Very funny!' replied George sarcastically, 'Knowin' yew, yew probably think she lives there!'

'Who …?'

'Wha' d'ya mean, who – yew just said Jerry Hall, dint ya?'

'Yeah, oi said Jerry Hall, but wha's the *she* bit got t'dew with it, Jerry the mouse is a *he* – Tom and Jerry?'

'Oi hed a feelin' tha's wha' he meant,' grinned John.

George rolled his eyes, 'But anyway – surely yew must've heard of Mick Jagger's ex-girlfriend Jerry Hall?'

'Oh – its someones name is it? Well, oi don't know who his girlfriends are … or were – oi weren't intew the Rollin' Stones – oi was more in t'tha' crazy lot, Madness.'

'Tha' sounds pretty appropriate, roight this minute!' sharply replied George, agitated by Reg's lack of knowledge.

'Never moind boys …!' said John, 'oi've worked out wha' we need t'be lookin' for. It's not Tom and Jerry's house, it's not Jerry Hall's house – its Harvest House – as in harvest mouse. It's a huge place up on the left, past the Spa Pavilion. Oi hed tew deliver a box of supplies there once. It's a little bit of a walk, but not tew far.'

'Never heard of it,' replied George, shaking his head.

'Well, tha'll be somethin' new for ya agin, won't it? Any-way … are ya both ready for the next verses? "Commemorated on a metal plaque are our heroes of the skoies, add together the two dates, and it will help foind your proize. Another plaque close by, has but one build date tew read, the Town Hall facade, is the place tha' yew need." Roight – hev ya got all tha'?'

'Wha's tha' fa-sar word agin?' queried Reg.

'Fa-ssarrrrd, Reg …' replied John, 'its tha' French word agin – the front of the building.'

'Oi can't git with them fancy words, whoiy can't we just stick tew our English words? Oi can't see whoiy we need t'say a French word when we're English – front is good enough for me.'

'Oi went through all this the other day, Reg, or hev yew forgotten about it already?'

George voiced his opinion with a Noel Coward impression,

'Saying fancy words, makes one sound more intelligent and more dignified,' said George, before reverting back to his normal Suffolk accent. 'Oi can't be dealin' with all tha' fancy stuff – if words are comin' out of me cake'ole and someone can git the jist of wha' oi'm talkin' about, then tha's all tha' matters. Oi've got no heirs and graces!'

'Yew certainly int got any of those!' grinned John. 'Anyway, enough yakkin' about French words, oi thought yew wanted an oice cream, George?'

'Ahh, yeah, roight – we got a bit soide tracked there dint we – it's all the fault of Arthur Mullard in the back there,' replied George with a flick of his head in Reg's direction.

To George's amusement, Reg sat bolt upright like a confused Meerkat, not sure whether to be offended or not, as he didn't know who Arthur Mullard was either.

Once all three were out of the car, they made their way along a footpath to the promenade and then took a left towards the pier.

George was salivating at the sight of people walking by licking their ice creams and upped his pace, 'D'ya want an oice cream, John?' he asked looking round.

'Oh, cheers, yeah oi'll hev one – just a regular noinety noine will dew me, thanks!' George marched off ahead like one of those Olympic walkers with quick steps and elbows jutting out and was up in the queue in no time.

With George gone, it then enabled John and Reg to ease back into a relaxed dawdle, *'Tha's better!'* said John with some relief. 'Sometoimes George is like a bloomin' ferret, rushin' about here and there – oi get worn out just watchin' him when he's loike tha'.'

'My Aunty Whiskey used t'be loike tha' …'

'*Aunty Whiskey* – wha' sort of a name is Aunty Whiskey? She loiked a drop or two did she – it made her floiy around the house, did it?'

'No, no – it was nothin' t'dew with drink – she had a cat called Whiskey and when the grandchildren were small they associated her with the cat, so she became Aunty Whiskey.'

'Well, oi s'pouz it could've bin worse …' grinned John, 'it's a good job the cat weren't called Tiddles, otherwise it would've sounded like she wet herself all the toime.'

Reg grinned, then continued, 'As oi was a sayin' – she used tew whizz about a bit, dustin' and a hooverin' all the toime, upstairs, downstairs, she never stopped. They said she hed some sort of trouble with her typhoid or somethin'…'

'Oi think ya lookin' for the word thyroid there Reg.'

'Tha' int French agin, is it?'

'No Reg, not this toime …'

Just then, George called out from behind them both, 'Here ya go John – ya noinety noine!'

'Oh, cheers George ...' replied John as he stretched out a hand for the ice cream, then with shock, noticed what George was holding in his other hand, 'Flamin' Nora! – wha' on Earth dew ya call tha'?'

John and Reg were stunned as George was holding the tallest, whipped ice cream they'd ever seen.

'Oi put on the charm t'git this baby, oi can tell ya,' he said with a big grin and a wink. 'Double cone, extra, extra large with chocolate sauce and sprinkled nuts on one soide and strawberry sauce with hundreds and thousands sprinkled on the other – wha' dew ya think of tha' then?'

John and Reg looked at one another and then noticed that other passers-by were pointing at the monster ice cream and chuckling, 'It looks a little top heavy t'me,' remarked John, stepping back with a grimaced look. 'Oi think we'd better foind somewhere t'sit down.'

As John and Reg walked over towards a bench, George walked a little slower as he attacked the chocolate sauced side of the ice cream with gusto when, 'Whoa, whoa, whoa ...!' the strawberry sauced side started to wobble before breaking away, then fell to the ground with a splat.

On hearing George's cry, John and Reg turned round to see George with a stricken face as the ice cream laid splodged in the middle of the concrete promenade.

John and Reg couldn't contain themselves and just burst out laughing, and the passers-by that had previously seen the monster ice cream couldn't help but laugh too. And then, to cap it all off, a large dog appeared and licked up the whole mess in a matter of seconds.

'Well, the dog is enjoying it,' Reg quipped, but George was not amused, and walked off in a huff to the beach to finish off the remains of his ice cream on his own.

'Oh dear!' chuckled John, 'He won't dew tha' agin in a hurry oi don't reckon, dew yew, Reg?'

'Well, serves him roight, he shouldn't be s'greedy. At least the dog had a lucky treat.'

John and Reg sat themselves down on the nearby bench and began watching the busy goings on along the promenade, while also giving the occasional surreptitious glance over at George to see how he was fairing.

'Dew ya reckon the ice cream has cooled him down yit?' chuckled Reg.

'Who knows – we'll probably not hear tew much from him for the rest of the afternuun, knowin' him,' replied John with a chuckle. 'Well oi'm enjoyin' moiy oice cream, all the same.'

Five minutes later, after the ice creams had been devoured, George slowly ambled over with a steely eyed look, 'Any witty remarks and oi'm soddin' off in the other direction, okay?'

John couldn't help but reply with the slightest of grins, '... Wasn't gonna say a word, George.'

'The Town Hall is just down there a bit, int it?' said George as he glanced down the road with a finger pointed.

John stood up to have a better look, 'It looks loike it. Oi knew it was along the front here somewhere – oi didn't realoise it was so near.'

'We moight as well git on with it 'en!' said George in a surly manner, having not quite got over the ice cream episode.

'Well, oi s'pose so – come on, up ya get Reg, let's see wha' we can foind this toime.'

Some 200 yards north along the road from the pier, the Town Hall prominently stands out as it is the only red bricked building close to the road. As with most Town Halls the entrances are usually quite elaborate and this one is of no exception.

On reaching the building, the lads found three commemorative plaques; one of marble – several feet away to the left of the doorway – and then two other, very different plaques close by to the right.
'What've we got up here?' said George looking up at the marble plaque, "In honoured memory of the crew of Lancaster LM two foive eight H A dash Q which crashed intew the sea in view of this place on August twenty fifth, noineteen forty four". Oi can't say oi've ever sin this afore, oi never knew a Lancaster bomber went down near here!'
'Oi can't say oi did either,' replied John. 'As oi keep sayin', this is openin' our oiyes to these things.'
'Is tha' another date for the book?' asked Reg.
'No, oi don't think it is, Reg,' replied John. 'There are two other plaques over here on the roight, and one of them needs t'be a metal plaque.' John takes a closer look and recites the writing on a metal plaque: "In commemoration of a long and happy association between the Royal Air Force, Felixstowe and the townspeople, noineteen thirteen tew noineteen sixty two", this is the one we want! A lot of people don't realise tha' Felixstowe had an air force base with floiyin' boat planes out on the Landguard end of town. There's a lot of history there – yew want t'look it up sometoime.'
'Is tha' roight … well, even oi dint know about tha' either?' George replied with surprise.
'Nor me …' said Reg, as he pointed at a stone plaque nearer the door. 'Dew we need this other plaque here?'

'Yeah Reg, we dew need tha' one tew ... tha's the construction date of this hall, if ya care t'read it all.'

As John jotted down the dates in the book, Reg muttered his way through the writing on the plaque until he reached the date and proclaimed, "... eighteen noinety two – its eighteen noinety two, John!'

'Oi've already jotted it down, thanks Reg.'

'It's a good job they didn't hev to reloiy on yew in the war, Reg,' remarked George, 'by the toime yew relayed any important message through to HQ, it would've all bin over bouy the toime yew sent it!'

Reg just turned and sneered at George, then gestered with a two fingered victory sign before slowly turning his hand round the opposite way.

'Well boys tha's another two more words on the grid,' smiled John. 'We've just got two more dates t'foind; one a little way up here, somewhere on Harvest House, and then tew finish off – Landguard Point. Come tomorra, we won't know wha' t'dew with ourselves after all this trekkin' about we've bin dorn the last few days?'

'Oi've still got a shed to paint, if the weather stays foine,' commented Reg.

'Tha' sounds excoitin' ...' said George with doleful sarcasm. 'We could've bin sortin' out a heap of stash and addin' up wha' money we could've bin makin' – it moight've changed our loives!'

'Flippin' heck, George – yew were hopin', weren't ya!' laughed John. 'Talk about being optimistic ...'

'Well, oi always say, ya always gotta look on the broight soide of loife, int ya ...!' replied George.

'Loike ya did when ya oice cream plopped on the ground. Ya still hed the other half tew eat, dint ya!' joked Reg, daring to have a dig.

George gave Reg a surly look and pointed a finger as a warning to mind his words, but Reg just gave a wry smile and looked out to sea.

As they slowly moved off, John had a quiet smile of his own and was half expecting a backlash from George, but fortunately this time it didn't happen.

'How far away is this Harvest House 'en?' George asked.

'Well – ya see the Spa Pavilion up ahead; it's beyond tha' about half this distance agin – so it's a bit of a walk,' replied John.

'Oh, roight …' replied George, 'if it's a bit of a walk, we'd better git gorn 'en,' and upped his pace and marched off before John had time to finish writing down the dates.

After a less than casual walk that John and Reg would've preferred, they reached the spa gardens that eventually, after a short distance, merged into the seafront gardens. The lads then took a left and headed up to the Cliff Top Cafe, where a pathway would then lead them on to some steps that would ascend to a road.

After climbing to the top of the steps, Reg was out of breath and puffing like a train, 'Cor … flippin' heck … these steps hev finished me off now!' he said with a face glowing like a beetroot.

George had no signs of being out of breath at all and stood, chest out with his hands on his hips like he had just conquered Mount Everest, 'Wha's the matter with ya man? Ya walk up a few steps and sound loike someone of a hundred and two!'

'We int all mountain goats loike yew, ya know …!' remarked John, who was marginally out of breath. 'And besoides, wha' if we are out of breath, we int exactly young'uns anymore!'

'Well, oi still feel young,' smugly replied George.

'Oi still feel relatively young tew, but oi int gonna give meself a heart attack troiyin' t'show it!' replied John sharply.

After a minute or so, they then steadily made their way left up the slight incline to Harvest House not uttering a word, but once they had reached the open forecourt to the entrance of the building, all three looked up in awe of its size.

'Bloomin' Nora, it's huge!' said Reg with his mouth left hung open.

'Yeah, it's quoite a buildin' int it,' remarked John.

'So if it int a hotel anymore, wha' is this place now?' asked George.

'It used to be Fison's headquarters after the hotel was sold off – obviously they must've moved on. Oi think they're all apartments now.'

'So when it was a hotel, d'ya reckon ol' Sam used t'come here and dew some of his handy work?' asked George as he looked high up at the windows.

'Very loikely, oi would've thought,' answered John, also looking upward. Then in a softer voice he continued, 'If he was anythin' loike tha' Raffle's bloke on the telly, it would've bin an ideal place t'nick some stuff. They dint hev the security loike they dew t'day.'

'Oi still can't imagine Sam dorn all tha', oi just can't,' said Reg as he shook his head again, still not wanting to believe it.

'Just think about it ...' enthused George, 'hoigh and moighty guests with jewellery, cuff links, cigarette cases, purses, wallets ...'

'*Keep ya voice down ...!*' interrupted John with a hushed voice and a look of horror on his face, 'oi hope nobody can hear yew roight now!'

'Nobody is listenin' t'me ...'

'We don't know tha'! There's plenty of windows open up there roight now, if someone hears yew talkin' loike tha' they'll think we're casin' the joint ...!'

'Oi'm off!' said a worried looking Reg, as he started to walk away.

'Just hold yew hard a minute, Reg ...!' said John. 'We int got the date yet. There's a plaque on the wall near the doors, oi'll just go and hev a look at tha' first – oi hev a feelin' the date we want is on there.'

John sheepishly walked over to the doors while Reg nervously looked about making things look even more conspicuous than ever. George just stood with folded arms and rolled his eyes.

Within no time at all, John had made his way back and was keen to move away from the building, 'Come on boys, oi've found the date, so oi don't want t'be hoverin' about here longer than we hev tew!'

Reg looked like something clockwork as he hurried his little legs back down the path towards the steps while George and John took a brisk, but steadier pace.

When all three had reached the steps together, John beckoned the other two to follow him down, 'Oi'm not writin' in the book in soight of anyone up there – if anyone was watchin' us, they'd definitely think we're casin' the joint if they see me makin' notes!'

George rolled his eyes once more before asking, 'So wha' was the date 'en?'

'Noineteen o three ...'

Once they had reached the bottom of the steps, they walked over to some railings to lean on as they overlooked the gardens.

'Yew two, dew make me laugh,' said George with a grin, 'yew always worry about wha' other folk moight be thinkin'!'

'Well, some of us hev got some scruples, unloike yew who don't seem t'give a monkey's about anythin' – Reg and oi loike t'go through loife without ... upsettin' anyone else or ... makin' a scene. Oi moiyself, loike t'get along quoietly with anyone and everyone ...'

'Loife is tew blinkin' borin' t'be dorn the roight thing all the toime! – oi loike t'make thing's interestin'.'

'Yew certainly dew tha' alroight, oi'll give yew tha'!' replied John with a look to Reg with rolled eyes.

'So where are we up tew with the words on the grid 'en?' asked George, 'not tha' it's gonna make tew much diff'rence.'

'Let's go foind a bench along the promenade and oi'll hev a look and see where we're at,' replied John. And then they all made their way down, back along the footpath.

As they walked along, George continued with his opinion on interesting lifestyles, '... Look at ol' Sam for instance, just think wha' an interestin' loife he must've had; visitin' all them big houses, halls and mansions, *not forgettin' hotels*, up and down the county – oi almost envy him ...'

'Envy a man who did criminal activities?' exclaimed John, 'Yew must be soft in the head!'

'Think about it – the plannin', travellin' in the dark tew a huge house, the darin' of breakin' in, achievin' the goal of baggin' the loot, the escape, the joy of your rewards laid out on the table ...'

'Not forgettin' the misery and despair tha' was left behoind tew the owners!' sharply replied John. 'It's interestin' when it's fiction on the telly but in real loife tha's a different matter. Whichever way yew look at it, it was wrong. No matter if ol' Sam was a noice ol' boy, it was still wrong!'

'Okay, it was wrong! – but he still hed an interestin' loife as far as oi'm concerned.'

'Well, the way oi see it, roight or wrong, oi loiked Sam, and oi'll always remember him as *oi* knew him,' said Reg with a smile, 'oi'll just pretend all tha' other stuff never happened, it int loike he murdered anyone ...'

'Not as far as we know?' said George with raised eyebrows.

'Oh don't start somethin' else, George, for croikies sake!' exclaimed John. 'Come on, let's sit down on tha' bench over there and hev a look in the book before oi go doolally!'

While John worked out the dates and numbers on the grid, George and Reg looked out onto the beach and watched the many families enjoying themselves playing in the sand with buckets and spades. One particular boy had caught Reg's eye.

'Look at tha' kid over there with the red hat,' he said with a chuckle, 'if he digs much deeper he's gonna disappear out of soight!'

As all three of them had a good chuckle at the size of the mound of sand that kept growing, Reg's eyes then drifted off into the sky as he went into his pondering mode once again.

'If oi dug a hole roight here b'twin me feet and kept gorn straight down through the middle of the Earth, oi wonder where oi would come out the other soide – d'ya reckon it would be Australia?'

'Here we go agin,' said George, with rolled eyes at John. 'Oi think he'd hev a bit of trouble gitting through the molten lava, don't yew, John ...?'

'Oi dew know tha's down there ...!' said Reg, 'oi was just talkin' hypa ... hypateck ... hypa-necka-teffaly ...'

'Its hypa-theckaly, ohh – yew've got me at it now,' tutted John. 'Hypo-thetically is the word, hypothetically.'

'Roight, hypa ... anyway, as oi were a sayin' ... wha' was oi sayin'?'

'Diggin' a hole!' bluntly replied George.

'Oh yeah – straight down through the centre of the Earth ... where d'ya reckon it would come out?'

'Kylie Minogue's back garden ...' smirked George, 'not tha' she'd be tew happy about a big hole appearin' in her lawn, but her reaction would be worth seein' when she clapped her oiyes on your daft head as it popped out in t'view!'

'Kylie Minogue ...,' said Reg with an adoring smile, 'Oi'll start diggin' now,' he joked.

After a minute or so, John clicked the end of his pen and was ready to deliver his latest findings. 'Oi almost forgot tew add the Woodbridge dates, but this is where we're at. Woodbridge has given us the words, "treasures, by and is", and here at Felixstowe, the RAF plaque has given us the word "nor".'

'Nor ... not north?' queried George.

'No – nor as in neither or not of somethin'; it'll all come clear in a minute. We dew have some duplicated numbers, and Sam has added some extra notes where some figures have t'be added together, which are this Town Hall date and the date from Shotley, givin' us thirty seven and the word, "the". One of the notes here says we must take away the Felixstowe mouse clue number from the Landguard number, but tha's our next and last port of call.'

'Very funny,' said George sarcastically, nodding his head with a wry grin.

'Oh, sorry about tha, of course the port is roight besoide it, isn't it – its funny how things work out tha' way. Anyway – so wha' we've got now is: "under the boat floor yule foind treasures galore, part stone lead by lace is neither sea nor river the place", and then there's two more words tew add tew it.'

'Run tha' bouy me agin, John,' asked George.

'"Under the boat floor yule foind treasures galore, part stone lead by lace is neither sea nor river the place" ..., obviously the Christmas yule is a, "you will" – yew'll – tha' was just t'throw us a bit.'

'"Neither sea nor river the place,"' muttered George, 'So wha' it means is, the boat is not on the water, it moight be standin' or stored somewhere?'

'Well, it's a possibility – but sittin' somewhere for forty years untouched?' unoptimistically replied John.

'Well, wha' about those old barn foinds loike ya see on the telly ...' said George, 'loike when they foind old cars and motorboikes tha's bin hid up for years – it moight be sittin' about somewhere?'

'He's roight, John,' added Reg. 'Oi watch those programmes tew, they foind just about anything yew can think of!'

'Boats ...?' queried John with raised eyebrows.

'Errr ... umm – oi can't say oi've ever sin them foind a boat ...'

'Oi can't say oi hev either, come t'think of it,' added George.

'Well ...,' said John. 'For the moment, oi s'pose we should look on the positive soide and not rule out tha' there moight be a very, very, slim possibility tha' it could still be out there somewhere, so ... oi recommend ... tha' we get back tew the car and git gorn t'Landguard without delay, don't yew? – come on, boys,' and with that, John was up and away off the bench with two happy followers.

As they walked back along the promenade, George queried the verse again. 'There was a bit yew said, John; part stone lead by lace – wha's tha' all about, hev we got the roight words there?'

'Oi was just thinkin' about tha' tew! We've got the roight words alroight, but oi think ol' Sam purposely threw in some odd words here and there tew troiy and throw the reader intew thinkin' they were somethin' else.'

'How d'ya mean?' queried George.

'Well, loike the word yule he used, some words can look loike one thing and can be said to sound loike another – and we now know it's definitely a yew'll as in you-will. Now with the lead word, it isn't a "lead the way" lead, and it isn't the soft metal lead either, so oi reckon it's mean't tew sound loike led but t'look loike either one when anyone first take a look at the grid.'

'But wha's the point of tha'?' asked Reg.

'It's probably t'stop someone guessin' some of the verse without lookin' for all the dates. Yew could've bin thinkin' tha' the stash was hidden under some sheets of lead, but without all the roight words said in the roight order ya never gonna solve this puzzle properly, are ya?'

'So wha' does, "the part stone led by lace" mean 'en?' asked George.

'Oi reckon …' said John, 'the stone has got t'be led by lace – by puttin' the lace infront of the stone tew give us lacestone.'

'Lacestone … Leiston – it's gotta be Leiston!' exclaimed George. 'Leiston is a bit inland innit – tha's not besoide the sea or a river though, is it?' he queried.

'Oi'm not sure whether it's near a river or not, George. It sounds loike we've got the roight place but oi'll hev t'look on a map t'be certain.'

Now, with a more positive attitude, their hopes were rekindled, and the lads were keen to get to Landguard Point.

Landguard Point

Landguard Point is an area of land steeped in history, as it's a strategic location at the mouth of both the Felixstowe and Harwich harbours.

Various fortifications from the 17th century onwards were built there and steadily improved upon over the years, until eventually Landguard Fort became the large stronghold that we see today.

Disbanded in 1956, the fort found a new lease of life by a team of enthusiasts in the 1980's, and is now a very popular attraction to the area.

Adjacent to the fort, the land seen laid waste, that stretches out to "the Point", is now an open nature reserve for all to visit. For migrating birds, this small piece of land is a busy stopping place from either direction and has seen many unusual species over the years.

The area was once home to RAF Felixstowe, and the Marine Aircraft Experimental Establishment, where flying boats and marine air-sea rescue and torpedo boats were in operation.

Today, the Port of Felixstowe dominates the area, being Britain's biggest and busiest container port and also one of the largest in Europe. Visited by around 3000 ships a year it plays a pivotal role in the movement of the UK's trade.

Having travelled just a few minutes down the road, the lads pass the Suffolk Sands Holiday Park before taking a left onto Viewpoint Road, where on route; several plastic, speed restricting road humps await the many visitors that frequent this busy location.

'Steady on John, moind the humps!' warned Reg.

'Okey dokey, Reg, oi've got it *all under control* – there shouldn't be any bashin' of heads on the roof liner today ...'

'Oi loike the way Reg warns yew John, when it int really necessary,' griped George, 'its couz moiy car is an old banger and John's is newer, is it Reg?'

'No – the other day was different; it's just the way it was. T'day oi thought oi'd say somethin' as yew moaned at me last toime, so oi thought oi'd say somethin' t'John.'

'Yeah, Yeah, whatever ...' George replied, flicking his hand in a dismissive manner.

As they worked their way along the road, the huge cranes on the portside dominated the skyline to their right. To their left, grassy mounds and wild scrub of a nature reserve obscure the view to the sea.

After negotiating a gentle Z- bend, the very low structure of Landguard Fort came into view and with the nearby car park looking fairly full, John decided to park in the nearest available space he could find.

'It's a busy time of day here roight now, so oi don't think there's much chance of us parkin' up on the viewin' point – this'll dew us,' he said as he slotted into a space and switched off the engine.

'So this is the last date tha' we've gotta look for is it?' asked Reg.

'*Where are yew Reg?*' questioned George with disbelief, 'John said earlier this is the last one, or were ya still thinkin' about diggin' a hole t'Kylie Minogue's?'

'Yes Reg ... this is the last one and hopefully we'll get t'understand the final clue to this whole treasure trail of Sam's – which, to be honest oi've quoite enjoyed. Well anyway, listen tew this: "Near tew the water with fort tew the left and the docks tew the roight, above the in and the out, it should be in plain soight". So, we've got t'walk just round the corner on t'the other car park by the sound of it.'

'The cranes with the containers go in and out, so p'raps there's something up on one of them?' beamed Reg.

'So, wha' are we waitin' for?' said George keenly, 'let's git gorn and crack this beggar once and for all, oi say!'

After a short walk of 100 yards or so, the lads then stood to the left-hand side of the car park and looked across to their right at the massive cranes unloading an equally massive container ship moored up alongside.

'Ooh, oi'm gittin' tha' funny feelin' agin just lookin' up at 'em,' said Reg with a shiver.

'Here we go agin,' tutted George with a shake of his head and then having a thought. 'Then agin – oi s'pose it must be a funny feelin' if yew've just taken on a new job here and marched up there for the first toime – especially if ya not use t'those sort o' hoights!'

'Standin' here, oi don't think ya realoise how big they really are,' commented John, 'for one; they're further away than wha' yew think, and two; there's a bloke now goin' up the steps – can ya see him on the second one along …?'

'Oh roight – flippin' heck, he dew look pretty small,' replied George.

'It would be interestin' just t'stand at the bottom of one, let alone cloimb up to the top of it,' added John.

'This fort here is more tew moiy loikin',' said Reg lookin' to his left. 'There's no hoights t'worry about on this place … hey … oi've just spotted somethin' – there's a date over there above a doorway, can ya see it?' pointed Reg.

John and George looked round to see a date inscribed on the lintel above a small doorway.

'"Above the ins and outs" – a doorway – well done, Reg. Oi think yew've found the last date!' smiled John.

"Eighteen seventy eight," recited Reg with a beaming smile, and then, slowly looking up to the sky, his eyes began to well up, '… now tha' we've found all of the dates, oi feel all sort of peculiar now we've come tew the end.'

'Oi think, Reg …' said John, as he lightly patted him on the shoulder, 'the word yor lookin' for is – is "emotional". All of this has bin quoite a journey for ya, oi suspect – even if it has been some forty years late!'

'Well, oi feel loike we've hed him watchin' down on us all this toime … Sam tha' is, as we've found all the dates tha' he set us out t'look for. Even if we never foind the treasure, at least oi feel tha' we did our best t'follow it through …'

'If ya feel peculiar now, Reg … can ya imagine wha' ya gonna feel loike if we dew happen t'foind it?' said George with great optimism.

'Steady on there, George!' replied John. 'Let's just keep this real for now, okay. We know there's a very slim possibility, but we've gotta keep our heads on an even keel for now and just take one step at a toime.

Let's get back to the car, and see if we can figure out the whole puzzle. We could be headin' back tew Leiston for all we know … unless of course tha's the name of the boat or somethin' – now there's a thought!'

Five minutes later they were all sat in the car; John with the black book rested against the steering wheel with pen at the ready; Reg leaned forward with elbows up on the backs of the two front seats, and George, vigorously rubbing his hands together in eager anticipation once more.

'First of all …,' said John with a momentary pause, 'we've got tew add up the Landguard numbers, which is … one and eight is noine, plus seven is sixteen, and eight more gives us twenty four, which on the grid is ... oh ... we've already got tha' one – it's the same number as we got at Woodbridge!'

'Are yew sure?' queried a slightly concerned George.

'Yeah, oi'm sure ...' replied John, and then he remembered, 'Oh, wait a minute, oi forgot, oi've gotta deduct the Harvest House number away from it, haven't oi? Let me see, where is it ... ah ... yes, it's thirteen. Thirteen from twenty four leaves eleven, which gives us the word on the grid, let me see – *dumpty, dumpty, dum* – "shed".'

'Shed?' repeated George.

'Tha's roight,' replied John, 'it says, shed – under the boat shed floor ...'

'WHA' ...!' George cried with disbelief, 'it's not in his boat then ...?'

'Yew mean ... the treasure is under a boat shed floor somewhere?' asked Reg, with his mouth hung agape.

'Its wha' it says here Reg – take a look for yourself,' beamed John, with a finger pointed on the page.

'WA-HOO!' bellowed George, excitedly. 'All the boatsheds oi know of hev bin around for years and years – so the stash has gotta be out there somewhere, it's gotta be! We're gonna be rich, Reg, wha' d'ya say t'tha' 'en boy ...?'

'*Whoa there, just hold on a minute!*' said John trying to calm George down. 'We've got t'work out exactly where it is first, so just hold yew hard a moment whoile oi read out the whole thing properly, okay!'

George and Reg vigorously nodded their heads, as they eagerly awaited John to recite the whole verse for the very first time: "Under the boat shed floor yew'll foind treasures galore, part stone led by lace, neither sea nor river is the place". Now tha's certainly put a different outlook on the whole situation, boys. There should be a map under your seat George, could ya fish it out for me please.'

After a quick rummidge, George produced the map and handed it over to John, who then quickly flicked through the pages at high speed. 'Here we are!' he said, as he slid his finger onto the town of Leiston, 'Tha' seems a bit odd?'

'Wha's odd?' asked George.

'Well ... hev a look for yourself. Leiston is roughly three moiles inland and the nearest river looks t'be more than two moiles away, so how can there be a boatshed there?'

George feverishly looked at the map in the hope of finding something that might help point the way, but he could find nothing.

'Oi'm flummoxed!' he said. 'It doesn't make any sense. If there int no water nearby how can there be any boatshed – unless, there's just an ordinary shed where a boat is kept in a garden somewhere.'

'If tha's the case it could be any shed amongst hundreds of others in Leiston,' remarked John, '- And wha' chance hev we got of foindin' tha' shed, even if it does exsist?'

For a moment, all three of them sat quietly thinking, when suddenly, John had a thought. 'Wha' if it isn't Leiston? It seems a rather long way, away to run about after ya stash if ya need any of it in a hurry!'

'It does rather,' agreed George.

With a slight frown, John then slowly turned round in his seat and looked Reg square in the eyes, 'Oi don't know whoiy oi've never asked this question afore, but tell me Reg – where about's did Sam live?'

'Tattin'stun ...!'

'Tattin'stun,' repeated John, 'as in Tattingstone?'

'Yeah – Tattin'stun ... if ya remember, oi used t'live nearer Stutton, before oi moved intew our village – Sam used t'live in a cottage about a moile down the road from me!'

John shook his head in disbelief, 'Oi just don' believe it, oi really don't ...'

'Wha's the problem, John? Ya look loike tha' Ipswich Town manager when they lose the match in the last minute of the game?' queried George. 'Wha's Tattin'stun got t'dew with anythin' – it doesn't sound loike Leiston does it?'

'It's the answer we're lookin' for, tha's wha' it is – tatting-stone!'

'Wha' are yew on about. How d'ya come t'tha' conclusion 'en?'

'Dew ya know anythin' about lace makin'?'

Both George and Reg shook their heads. 'Moiy Anne makes lace doilies as one of her hobbies, ya know, stitchin' and twistin' whoite threads t'make little frilly lookin' things to lay on tables and wha'ever – it does nothin' for me but she enjoys dorn it, but tha's besoides the point – anyway, through her dorn tha' oi dew know there's another word for lace makin', *and tha's tatting!*'

'So Tattin'stun is the place we need t'look,' exclaimed George, 'but surely there's no ...' and then it dawned on him, '– Tattin'stun Lake!'

'Exactly!' replied John, '"neither sea nor river", oi dint think of a lake!'

'Aah ... the boatshed on Tattin'stun Lake, oi can remember it now,' beamed Reg. 'So, does this mean John; it's where the treasure is – under the boatshed floor?'

'Well it sounds loike it and oi'm pretty sure oi'm roight – it all fits together perfectly. Oi just can't believe we never asked yew where Sam lived ...!'

'Or tha' Inspector Clouseau behoind us here never told us,' remarked George with rolled eyes. 'So wha' are we waitin' for 'en boys? Come on John, git this car started and let's git gorn!'

Full of enthusiasm, the threesome set off along the road back to town with just a little too much exuberance, as John caught a few speed-humps a touch too fast, causing his friends to jolt skyward on more than one occasion. With spirits on a high, not even George was going to complain this time.

Final Stop

Fifteen minutes later, they were over the Orwell Bridge and taking the first sliproad left off, onto the Brantham/Manningtree road. A further half mile along the road they then passed a sign pointing to Jimmy's Farm which caught George's eye, 'Hev either of yew two hed any sausages from Jimmy's Farm afore?'

'Oi can't say oi hev,' replied John, while Reg shook his head.

'Cor, they're really good'uns. It's got me mouth waterin' just thinkin' about them. Ya want t'pop down there sometoime, they dew some lovely stuff. Oi Reg – pass me moiy bag of pork over here a minute, will ya. Oi fancy a couple of bits after talkin' about sausages.'

Reg handed over the bag which soon had George delving inside. 'D'ya want some?' he asked, but both Reg and John declined on the offer. 'Did ya ever git t'hear about little ol' Mrs Treadwell at the butchers,' he continued, 'ya know ... the little ol' lady of about noinety foive and about foive foot nothin'?'

'Oh ... oi know who ya mean,' replied Reg.

'Well, ol' Fred was tellin' me tha' she use t'go intew his shop every week t'boiy just *one* sausage at a toime ...'

'One sausage?' queried Reg.

'Yeah, tha's roight, just one, single sausage. She said she had a small appetite and one sausage was all she could eat at a toime. She always stuck tew her old fashioned larder ya see, she dint hev a fridge or a freezer, so she couldn't exactly keep a pound of sausages for six or seven weeks, could she? Can ya imagine – toad in the hole with just one sausage sittin' in the batter, or "banger" and mash ...' he laughed.

As George delved into the bag of pork once more, he looked across at John to see that he appeared sloightly vacant, ' Are ya alroight John, yew seem a bit quoiet?'

'Oi've, umm ... just realoised somethin' ... and oi don't know whoiy oi dint think of it earlier – well – any of us really. It must've bin all the excoitment of solvin' the riddle ...'

'Realoised wha' exactly?' queried George.

'Well ... yew'll both realoise in a few minutes or so when we get there – it's not good!'

With John's remark, George turned round in his seat to see that Reg was equally as baffled.

After a few twists and turns they drive the final stretch downhill onto Lemons Hill Bridge, which has approximately 200 yards of white painted railings, spanning the reservoir known as Alton Water.

Alton Reservoir was officially opened by H.R.H. Princess Anne, in 1987 to supply the ever growing town of Ipswich, and the surrounding area. Today, it is now a very popular venue for cyclists, walkers, birdwatchers, water sport enthusiasts and families who like to spend their leisure time by the water.

John slowly pulled up to a halt in the middle of the bridge and then switched off the engine. Without saying a word, he then got out of the car, shut the door and then slowly walked over to the siderail. Both George and Reg seemed to be in slow motion as they followed suit.

With hands in his pockets, John looked out across the vast expanse of water. 'Ya realoise *now*, don't ya both?' he quietly said.

George gave a gentle nod of acknowledgement. 'Tattin'stun Lake doesn't exist anymore, does it,' said a dejected George.

'Oi thought the lake was on the other soide of the mansion,' said Reg with uncertainty. 'Oi can still see it in moiy moind as plain as day!'

'Yor thinkin' about the bit up the road and round the corner, Reg – it's still part of this!' replied John.

With a finger pointed out towards the water, John continued. 'If moiy memory serves me roight, the lake used t'be out there in the middle almost opposite the mansion – wha' wiv the floodin' of this whole valley, we're talkin' maybe twenty foot or more, deeper than wha' we can see it now – and the boatshed with it, which could be anywhere out there!'

'So tha's it then!' said George dolefully shaking his head, 'The end of the road and all for nothin'! All those flippin' dates and places, and we still end up with nothin' – oi can't believe it!'

John put his arm around the back of Reg's shoulder and gave him a comforting hug, 'Well, wha' can oi say Reg ... the passing of toime in this ever changin' world has beaten us on this occasion, oi'm afraid – fallen at the last fence and our proize has gone. But we troied our best, dint we?'

Although disappointed, Reg could still manage a smile. 'Its alroight John, oi'm okay about it. Oi've really enjoyed meself this week and learnt a lot of things along the way, which oi think tha's wha' Sam really intended for me – and besoides – even if we hed found Sam's treasure and made loads of money from it, oi probably wouldn't hev known wha' t'spend it on anyway!'

'Well, look at it this way, Reg – and you, George – we may not hev found the treasure, but we found a lot of wonderful treasures on our journey around our Suffolk county these last few days. So thanks to Sam, he's enriched our moinds – if nothing else!'

John shook Reg's shoulder like the good friends that they were and both grinned at one another before looking out across the water once more, while George, stood with a dead serious look on his face ... 'Oi've just hed an idea, boys ...!' he said with eyes alight. 'Wha' if we got ahold of some scuba doivin' equipment ...?'

The End

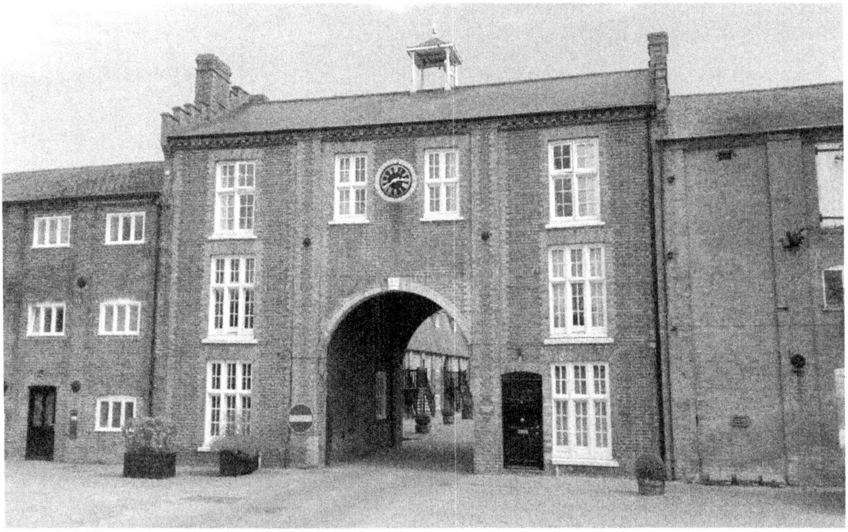

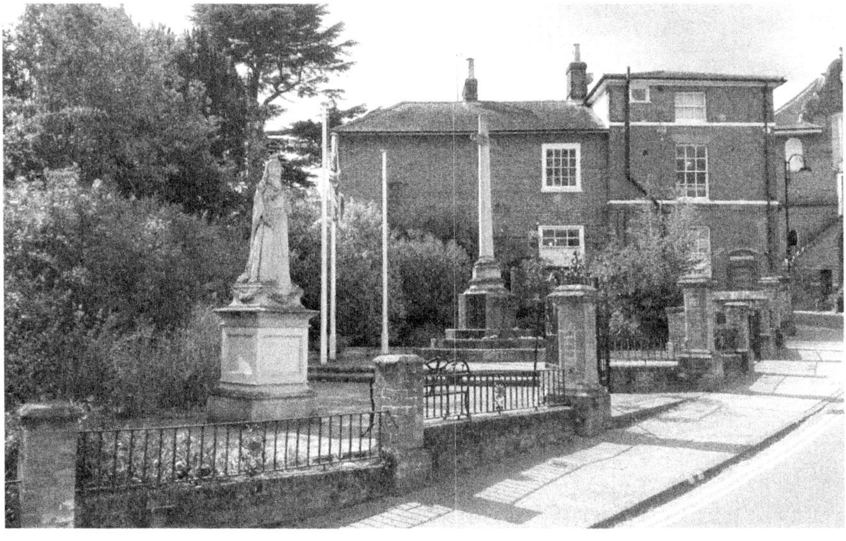

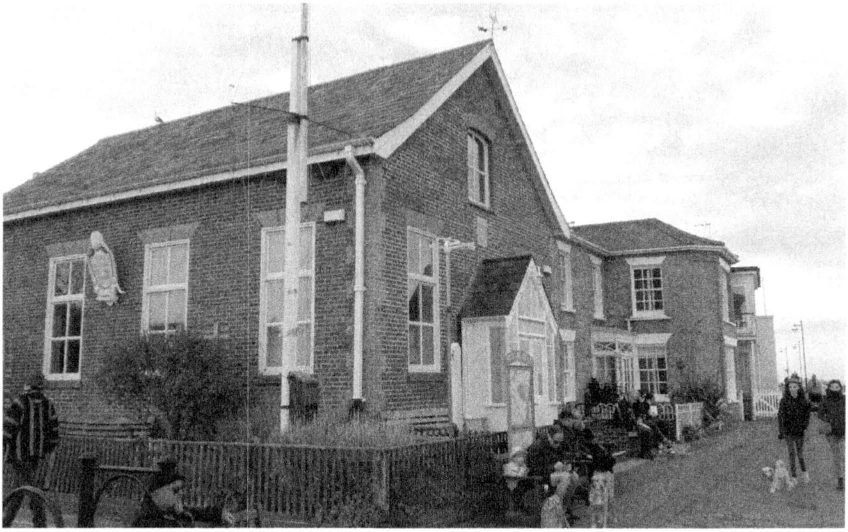

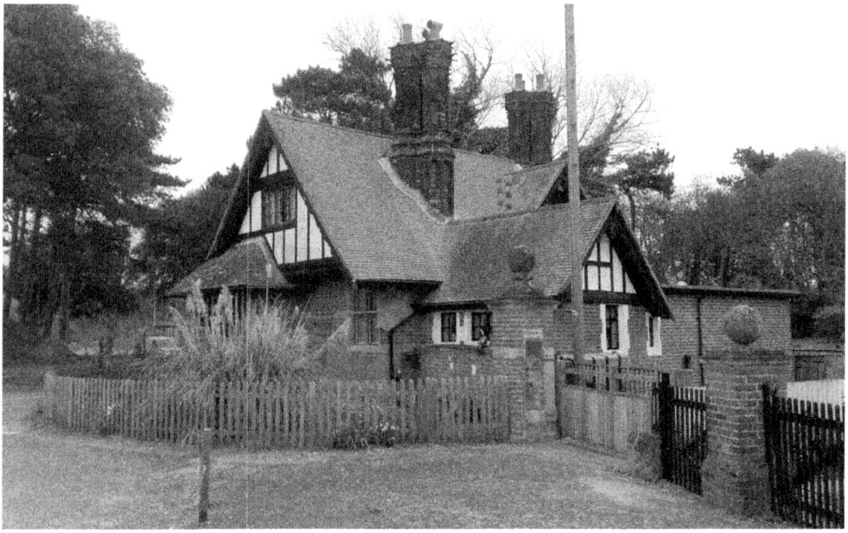

153

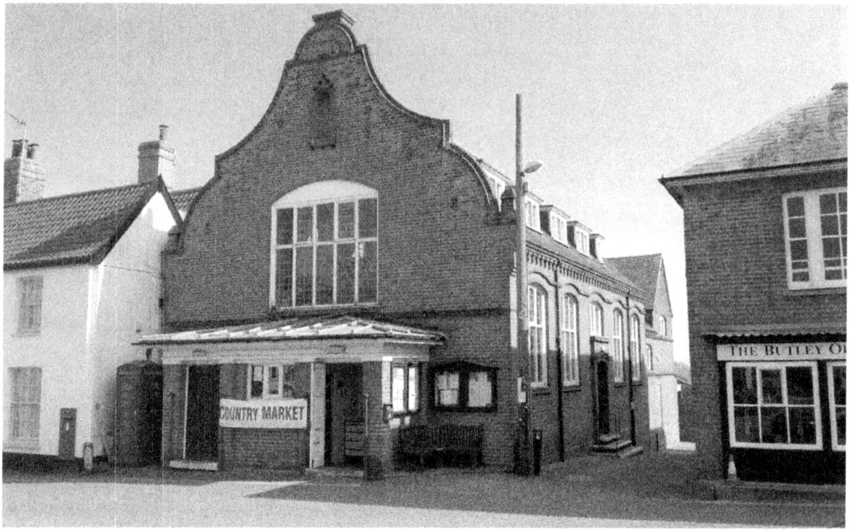
COUNTRY MARKET
THE BUTLEY O

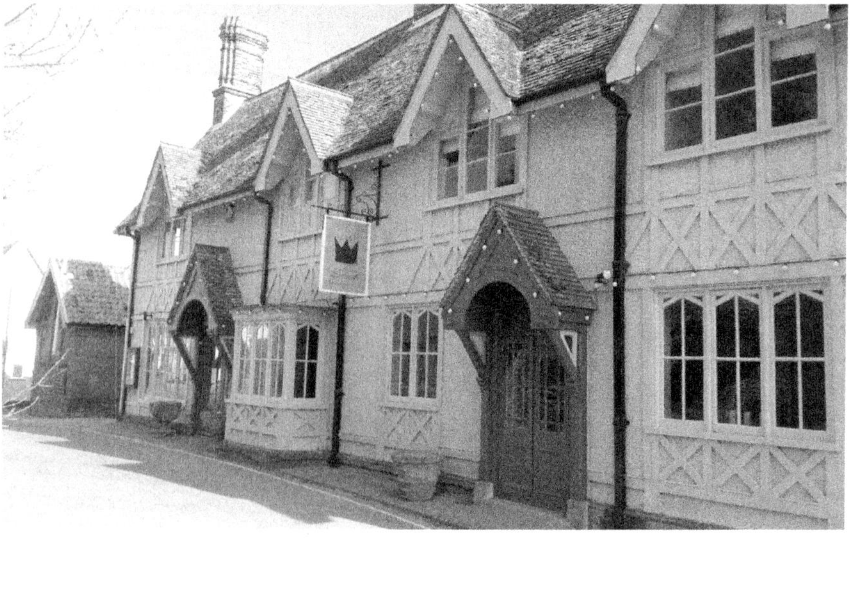

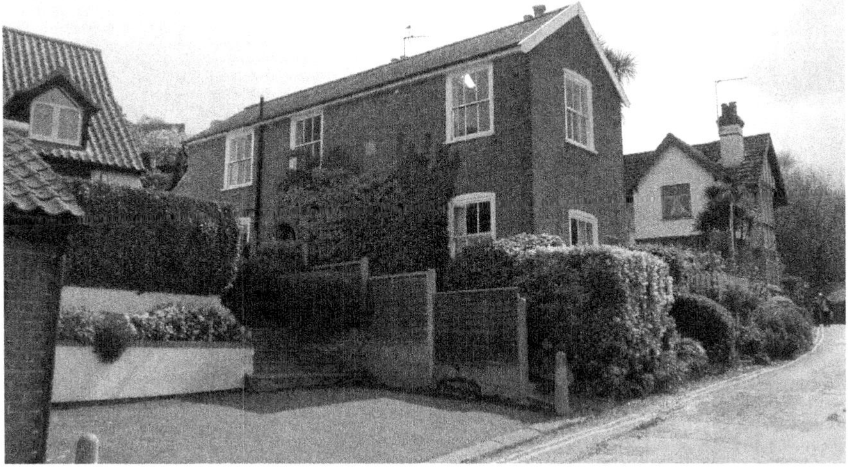

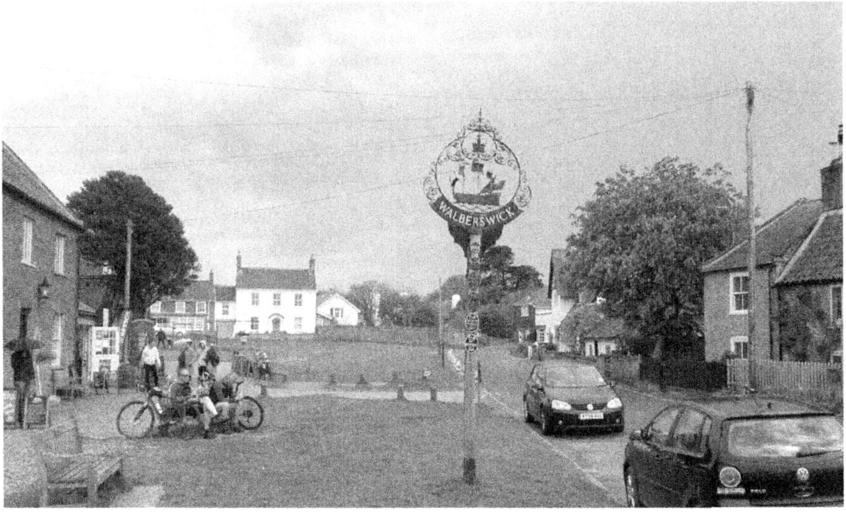
WALBERSWICK

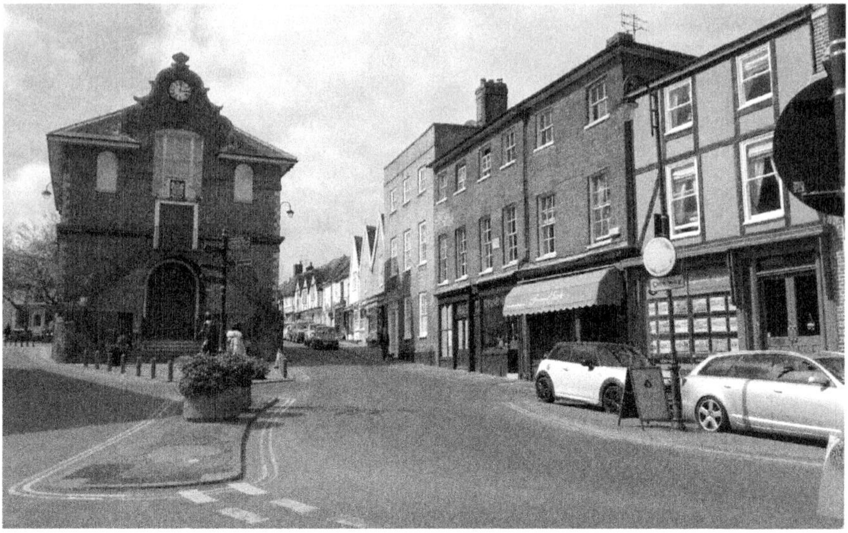

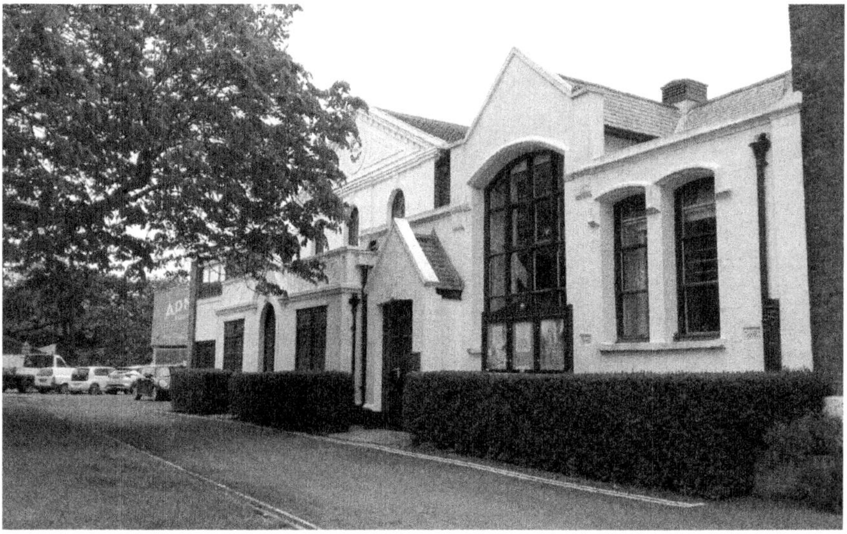

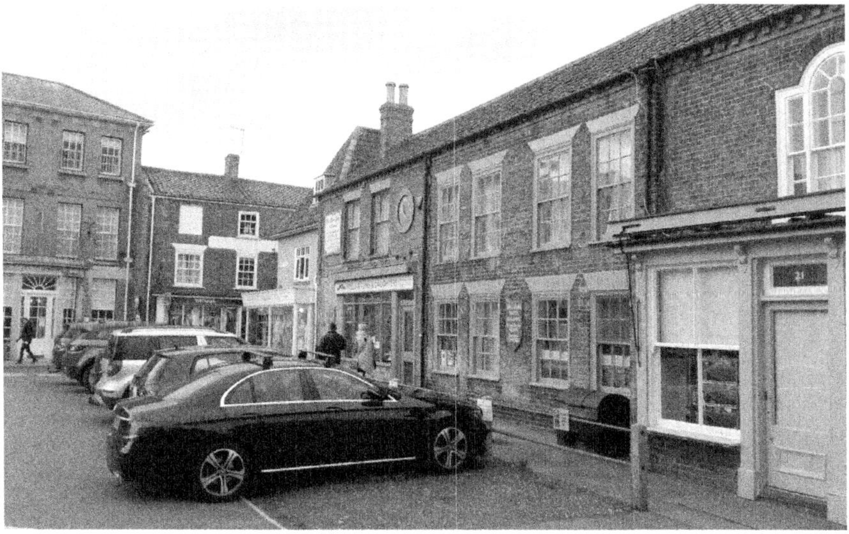
21

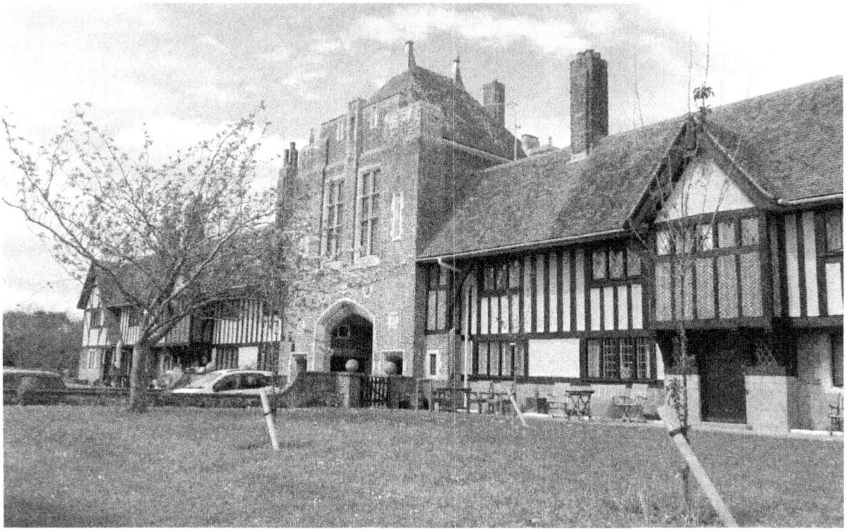

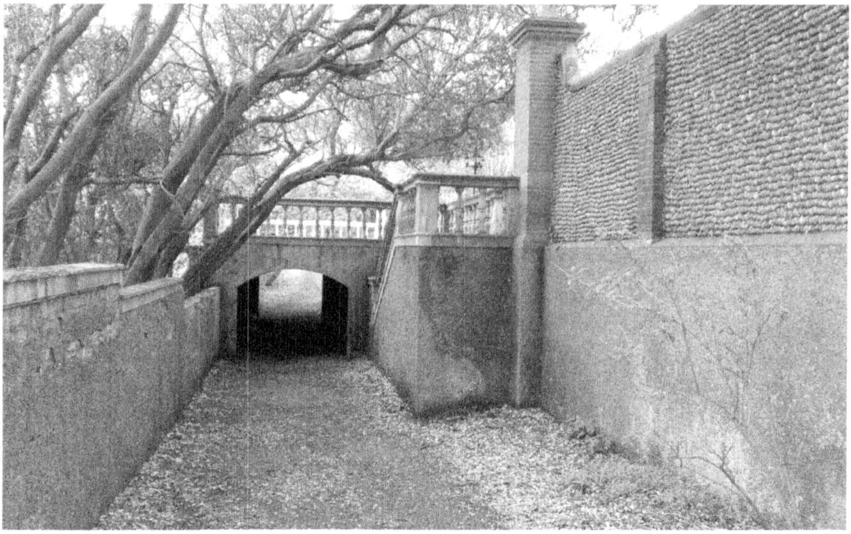

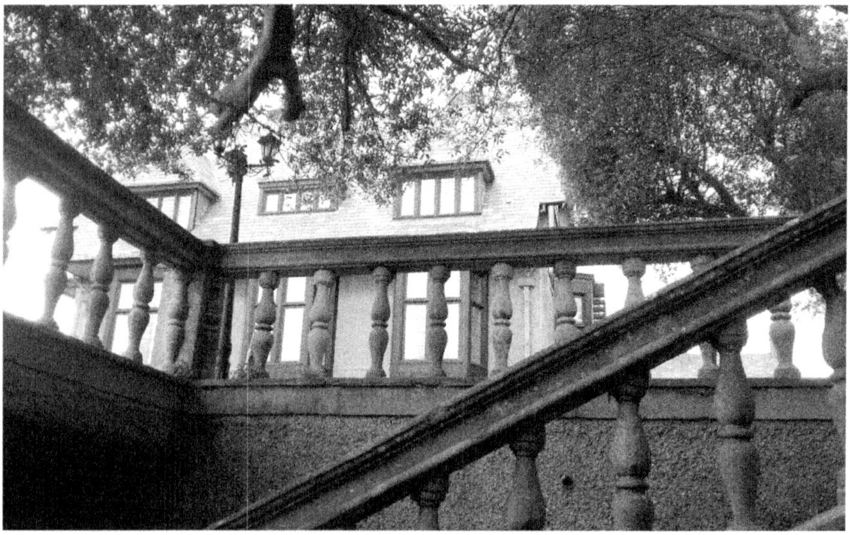

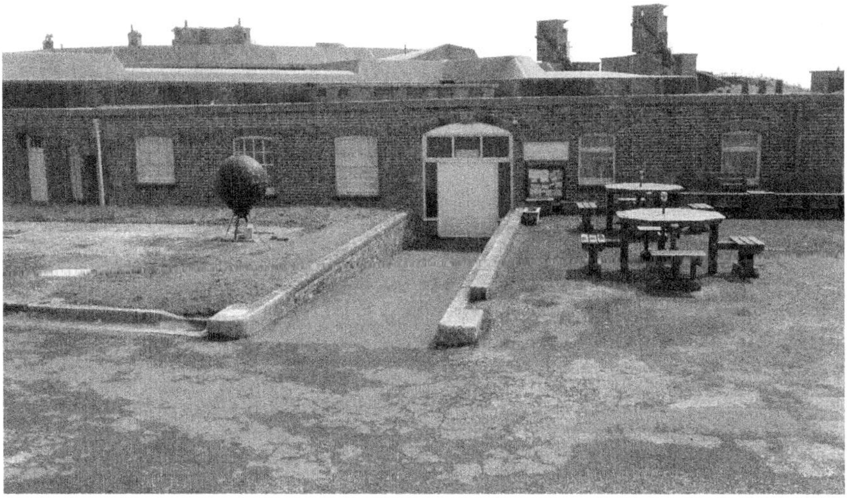

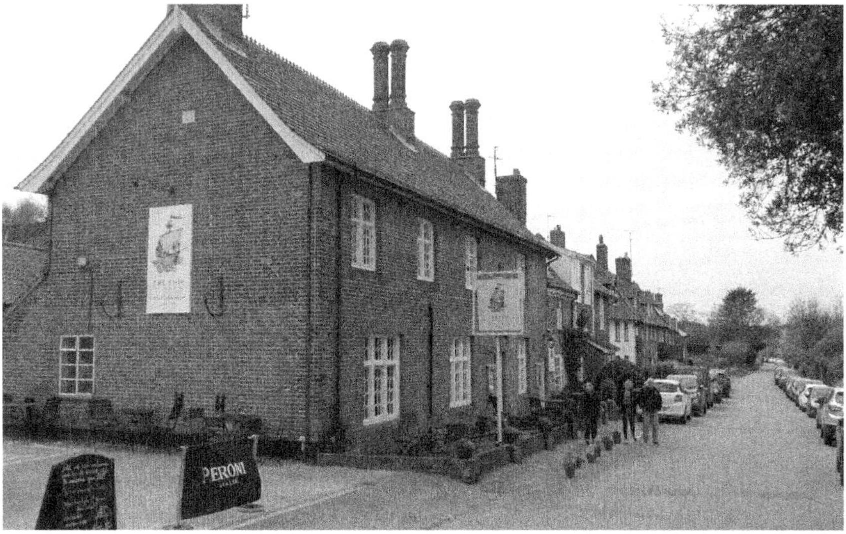
PERONI

160

161

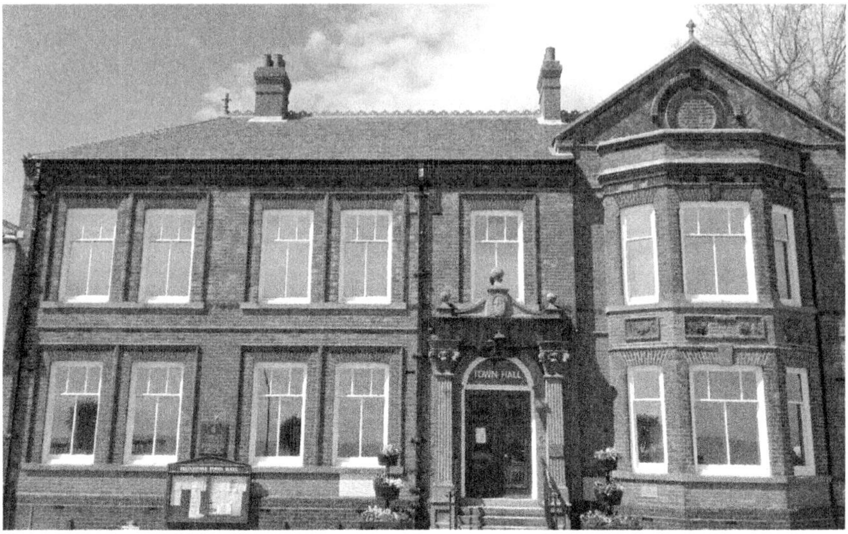
TOWN HALL

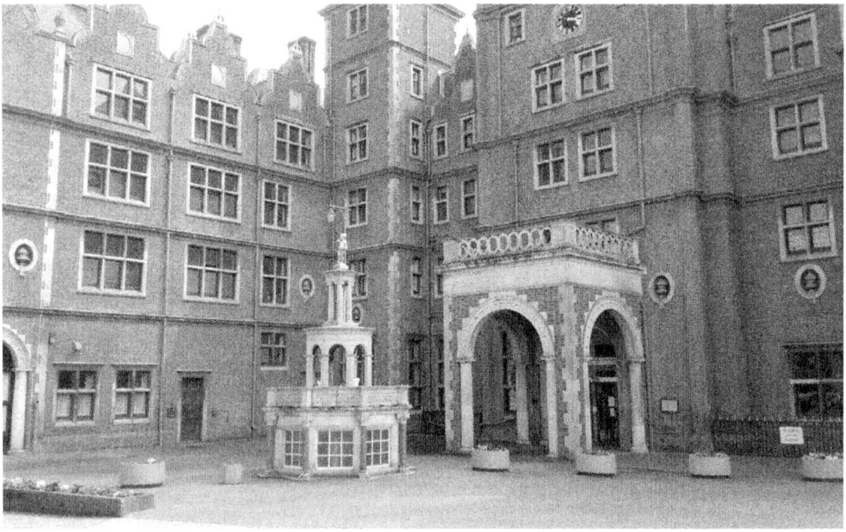

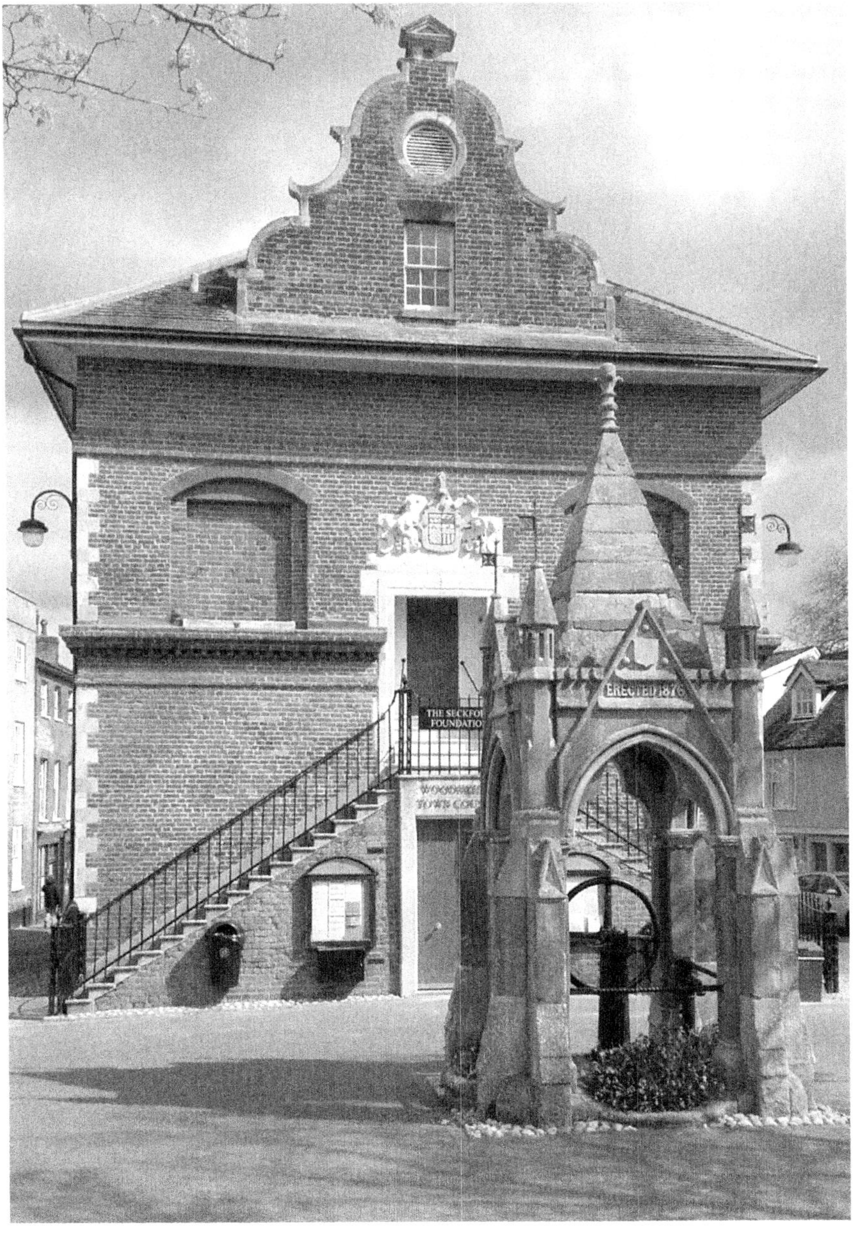

Identity of photographs in alphabetical order

	Pages
Aldeburgh	160, 161
Bawdsey	152
Dunwich	159
Felixstowe	162
Landguard Point	159
Orford	154
Pin Mill	155
Sizewell	158
Shotley	153
Snape	151
Southwold	152, 156, 157
Thorpeness	157
Walberswick	155
Woodbridge	151, 156, 161, 163

Printed in Great Britain
by Amazon